Clifford
The Big Red Dog
The Movie Graphic Novel

Adapted by **Georgia Ball**
Illustrated by **Chi Ngo**

Scholastic Inc.

ISBN 978-1-338-66511-6 (hardcover)

ISBN 978-1-338-66510-9 (paperback)

10 9 8 7 6 5 4 3 2 1   20 21 22 23 24

Printed in the U.S.A.　113

First printing 2020 • Edited by Samantha Swank

Art by Chi Ngo • Lettering by Rae Crawford • Book design by Betsy Peterschmidt

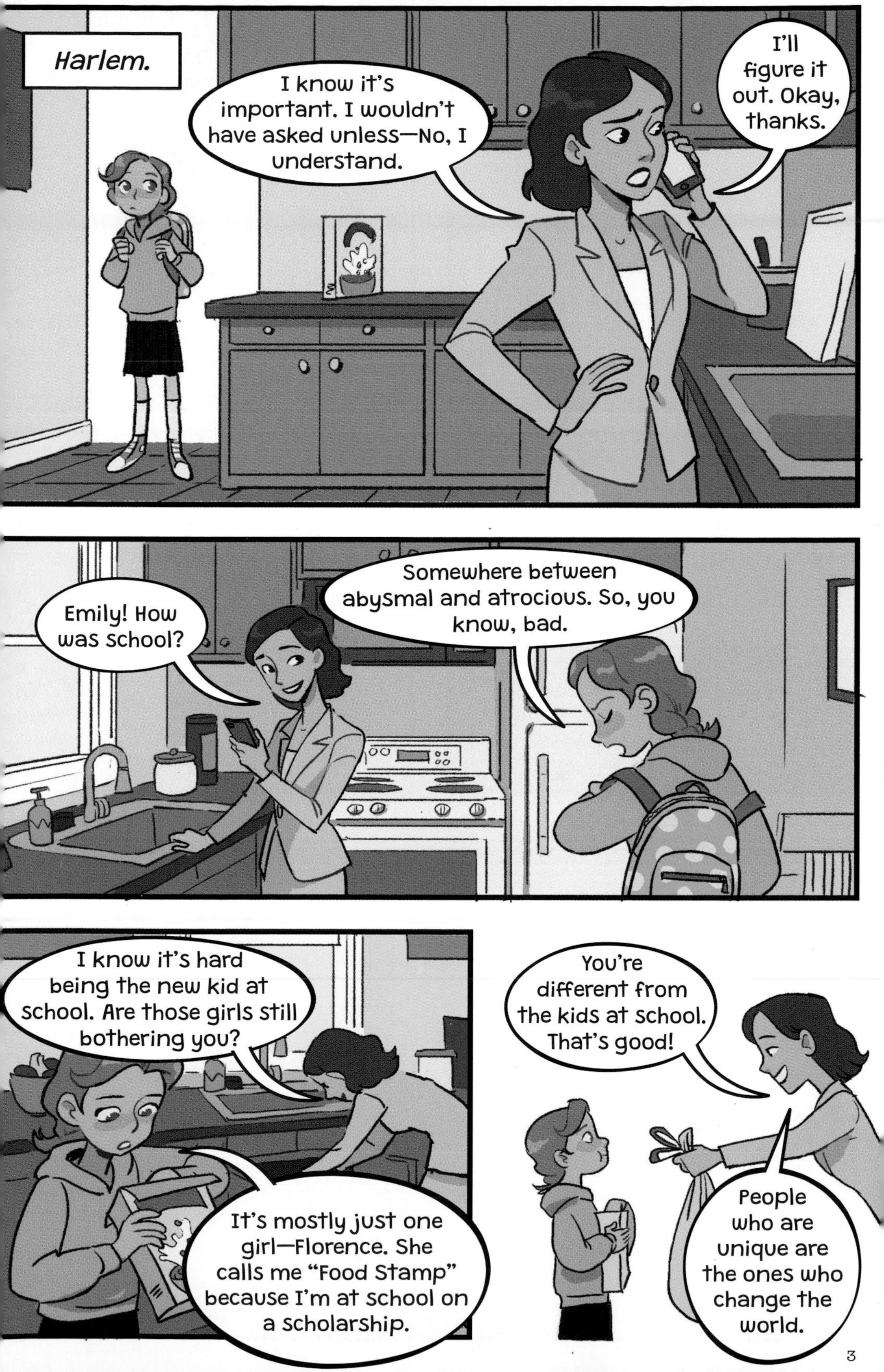
Harlem.
I know it's important. I wouldn't have asked unless—No, I understand.
I'll figure it out. Okay, thanks.
Emily! How was school?
Somewhere between abysmal and atrocious. So, you know, bad.
I know it's hard being the new kid at school. Are those girls still bothering you?
It's mostly just one girl—Florence. She calls me "Food Stamp" because I'm at school on a scholarship.
You're different from the kids at school. That's good!
People who are unique are the ones who change the world.

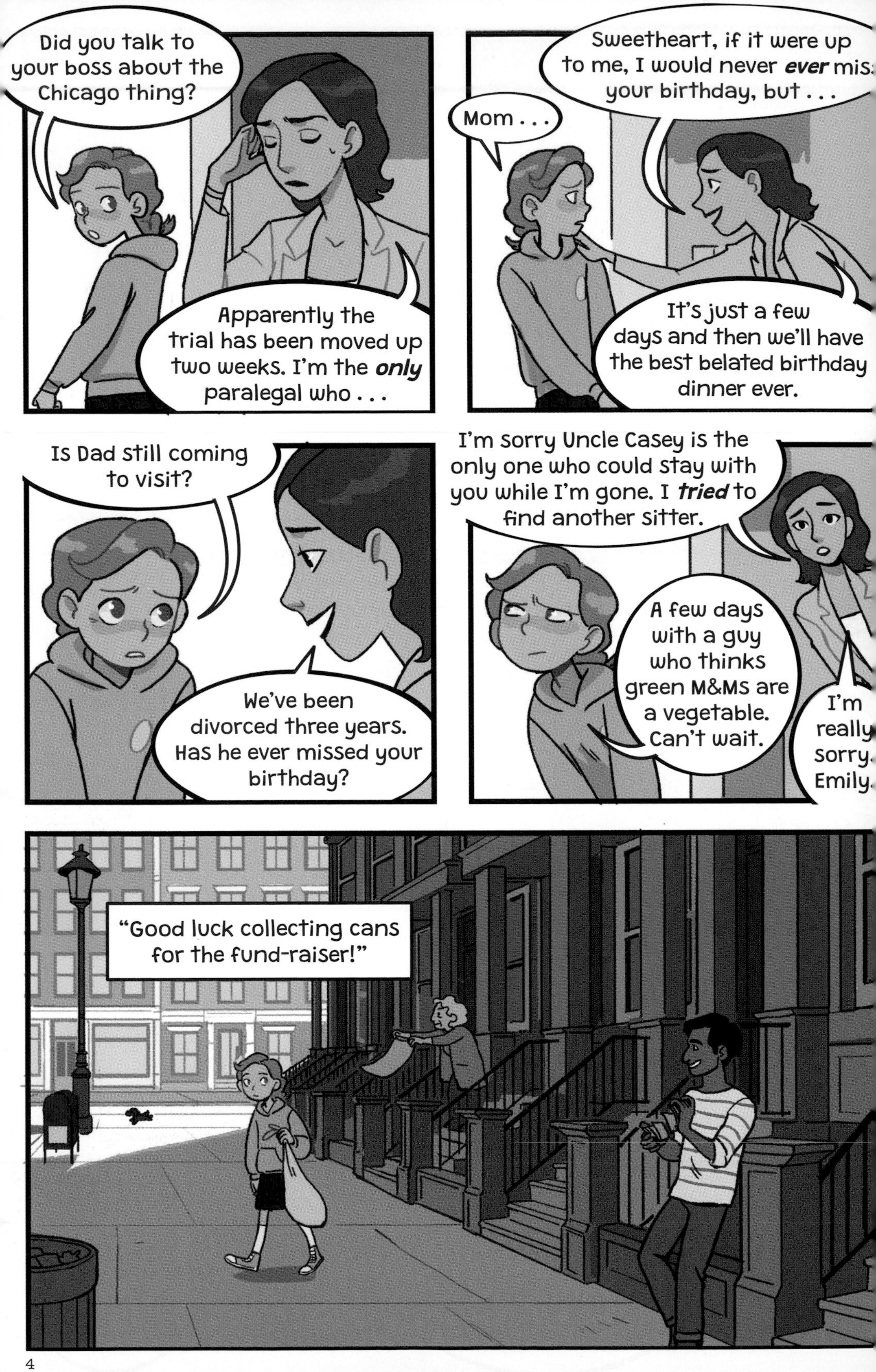
Did you talk to your boss about the Chicago thing?
Apparently the trial has been moved up two weeks. I'm the *only* paralegal who . . .
Mom . . .
Sweetheart, if it were up to me, I would never *ever* miss your birthday, but . . .
It's just a few days and then we'll have the best belated birthday dinner ever.
Is Dad still coming to visit?
We've been divorced three years. Has he ever missed your birthday?
I'm sorry Uncle Casey is the only one who could stay with you while I'm gone. I *tried* to find another sitter.
A few days with a guy who thinks green M&Ms are a vegetable. Can't wait.
I'm really sorry. Emily.
"Good luck collecting cans for the fund-raiser!"

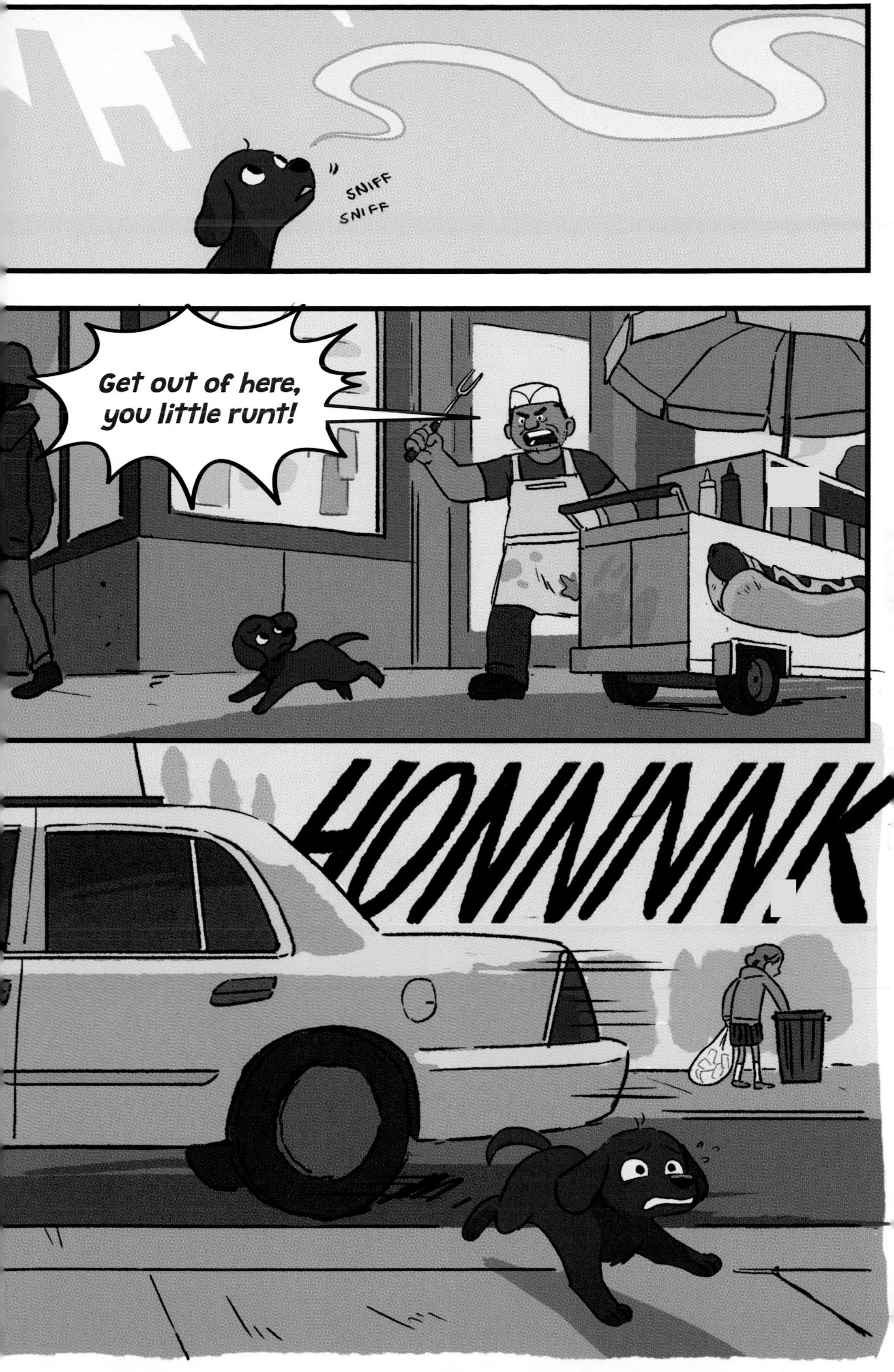
SNIFF
SNIFF
Get out of here, you little runt!
HONNNK

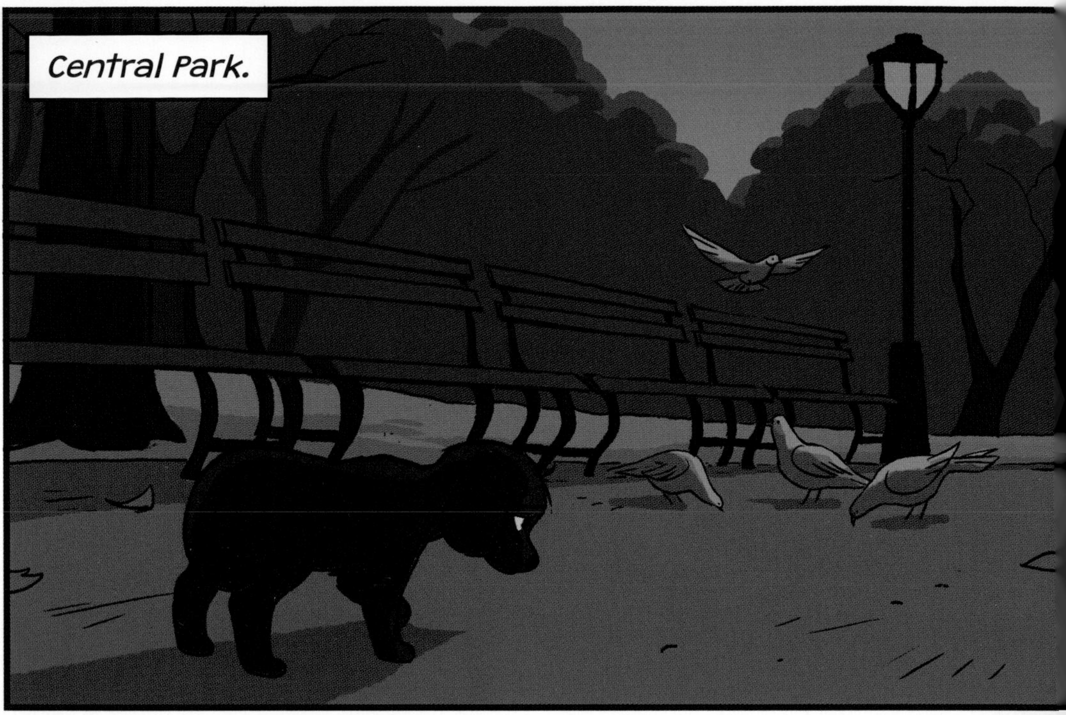
Central Park.

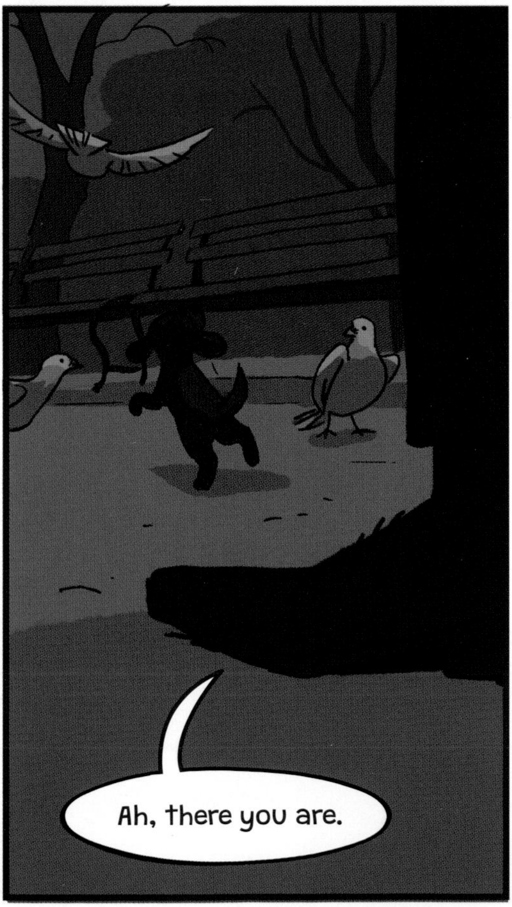
Ah, there you are.

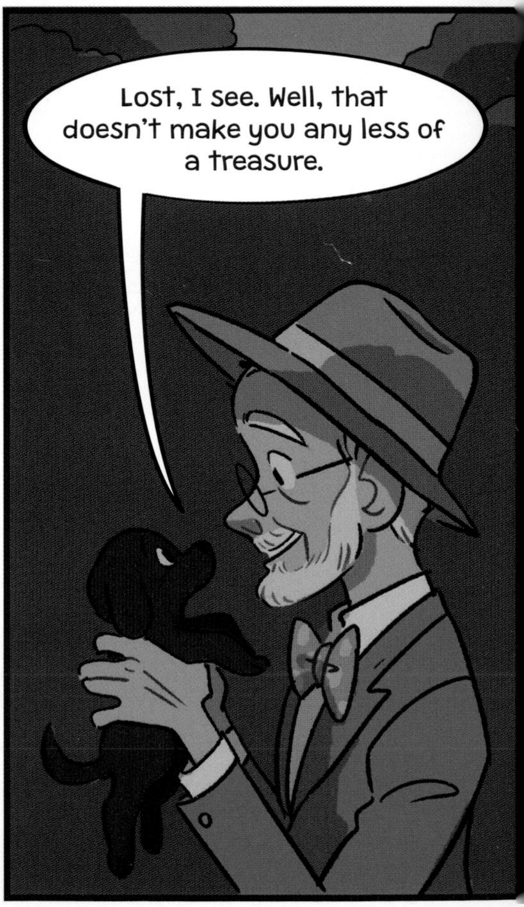
Lost, I see. Well, that doesn't make you any less of a treasure.

The next morning, Emily walks with her uncle to school.

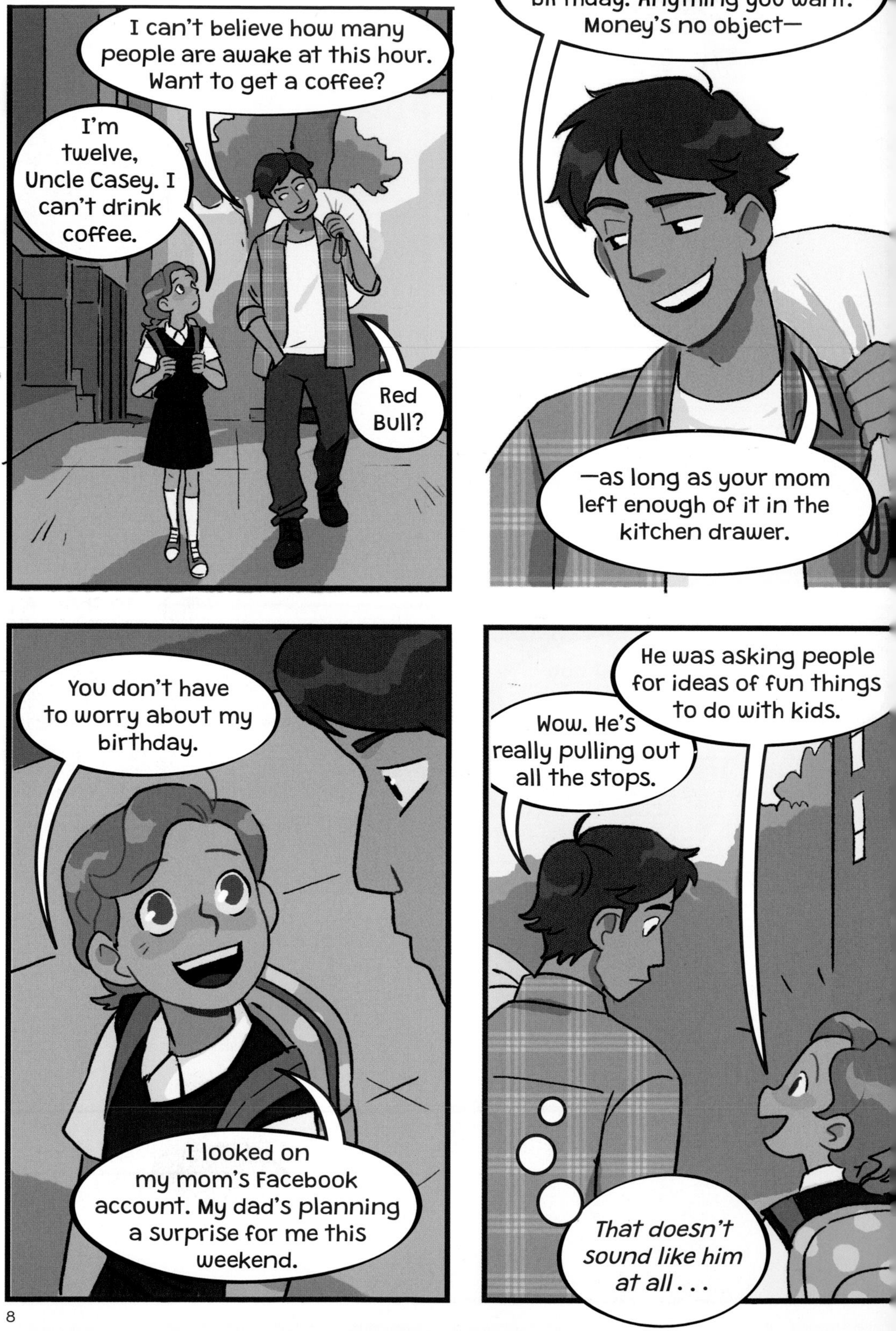
I can't believe how many people are awake at this hour. Want to get a coffee?
I'm twelve, Uncle Casey. I can't drink coffee.
Red Bull?
We're going to do something super cool for your birthday. Anything you want. Money's no object—
—as long as your mom left enough of it in the kitchen drawer.
You don't have to worry about my birthday.
I looked on my mom's Facebook account. My dad's planning a surprise for me this weekend.
Wow. He's really pulling out all the stops.
He was asking people for ideas of fun things to do with kids.
That doesn't sound like him at all . . .

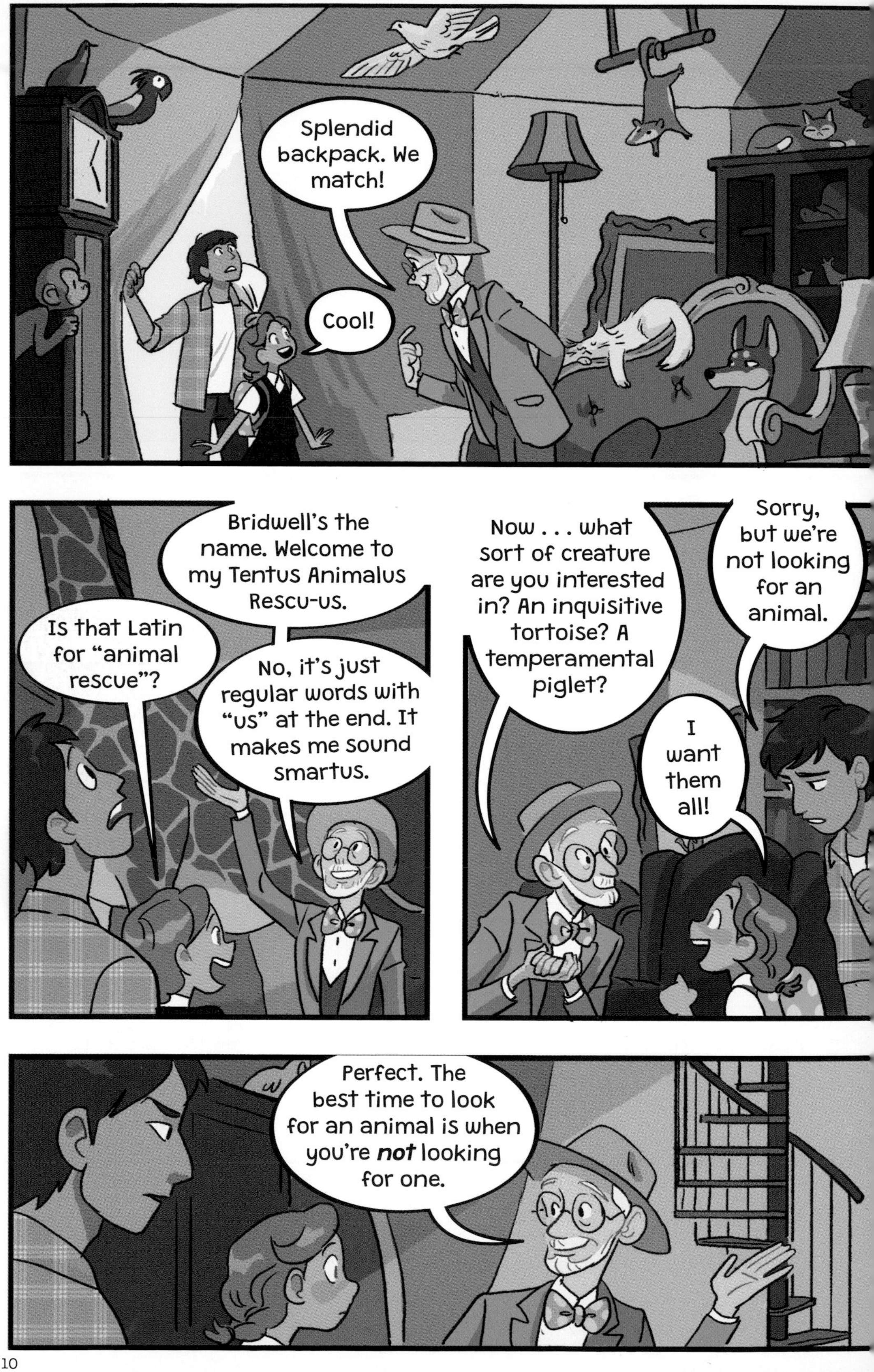
Splendid backpack. We match!
Cool!
Bridwell's the name. Welcome to my Tentus Animalus Rescu-us.
Is that Latin for "animal rescue"?
No, it's just regular words with "us" at the end. It makes me sound smartus.
Now . . . what sort of creature are you interested in? An inquisitive tortoise? A temperamental piglet?
Sorry, but we're not looking for an animal.
I want them all!
Perfect. The best time to look for an animal is when you're ***not*** looking for one.

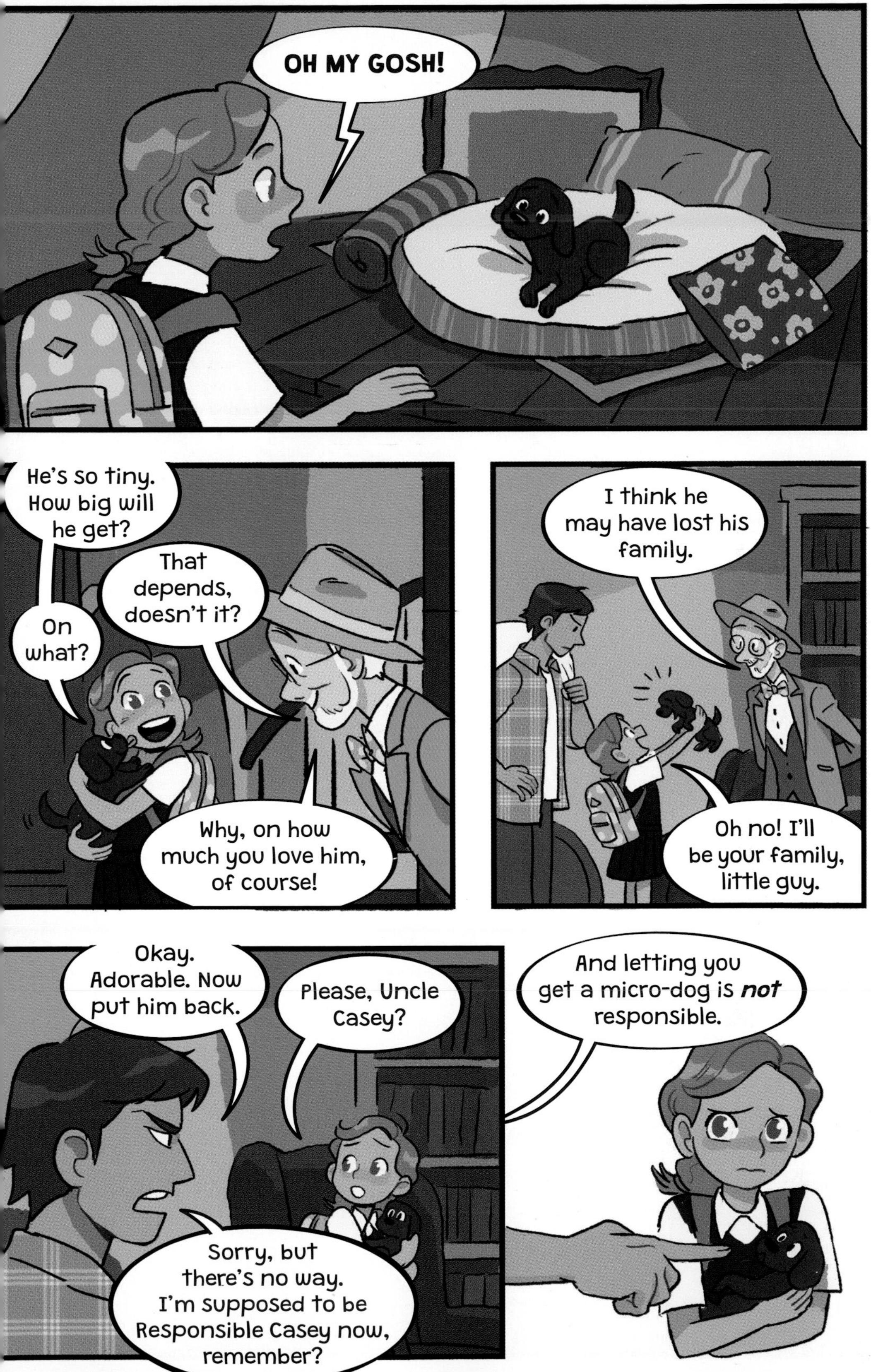
OH MY GOSH!
He's so tiny. How big will he get?
That depends, doesn't it?
On what?
Why, on how much you love him, of course!
I think he may have lost his family.
Oh no! I'll be your family, little guy.
Okay. Adorable. Now put him back.
Please, Uncle Casey?
Sorry, but there's no way. I'm supposed to be Responsible Casey now, remember?
And letting you get a micro-dog is *not* responsible.

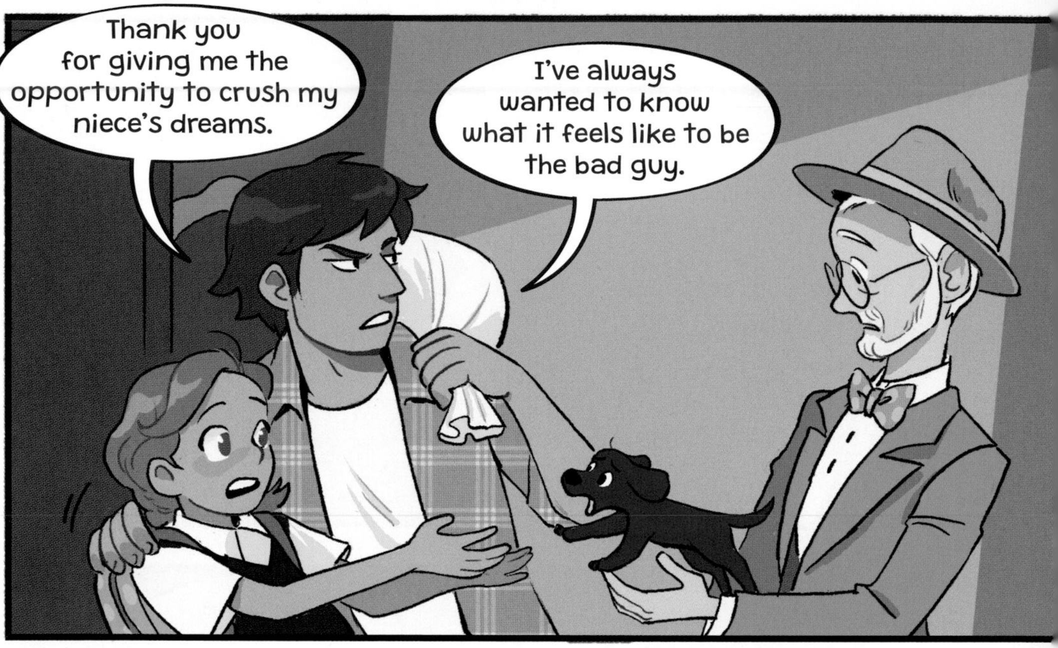
Thank you for giving me the opportunity to crush my niece's dreams.
I've always wanted to know what it feels like to be the bad guy.

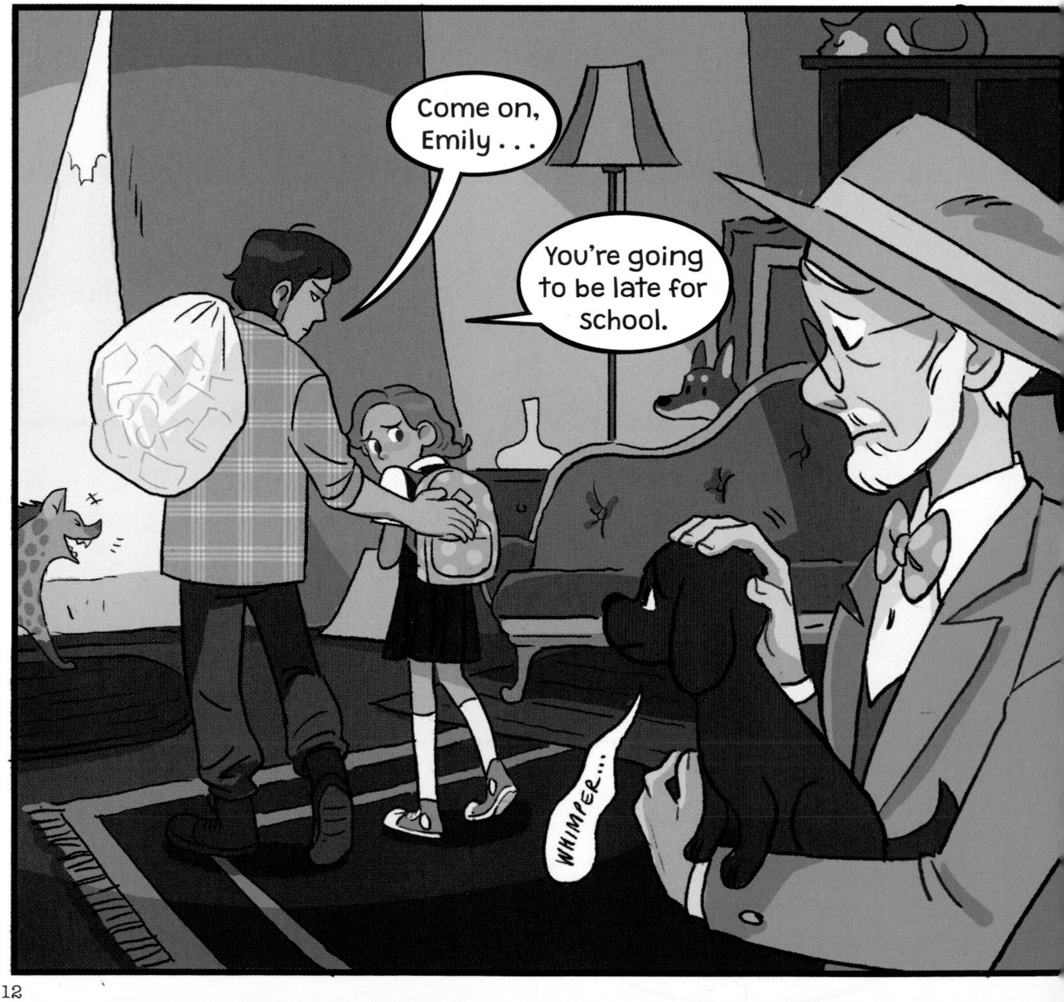
Come on, Emily . . .
You're going to be late for school.
WHIMPER...

14

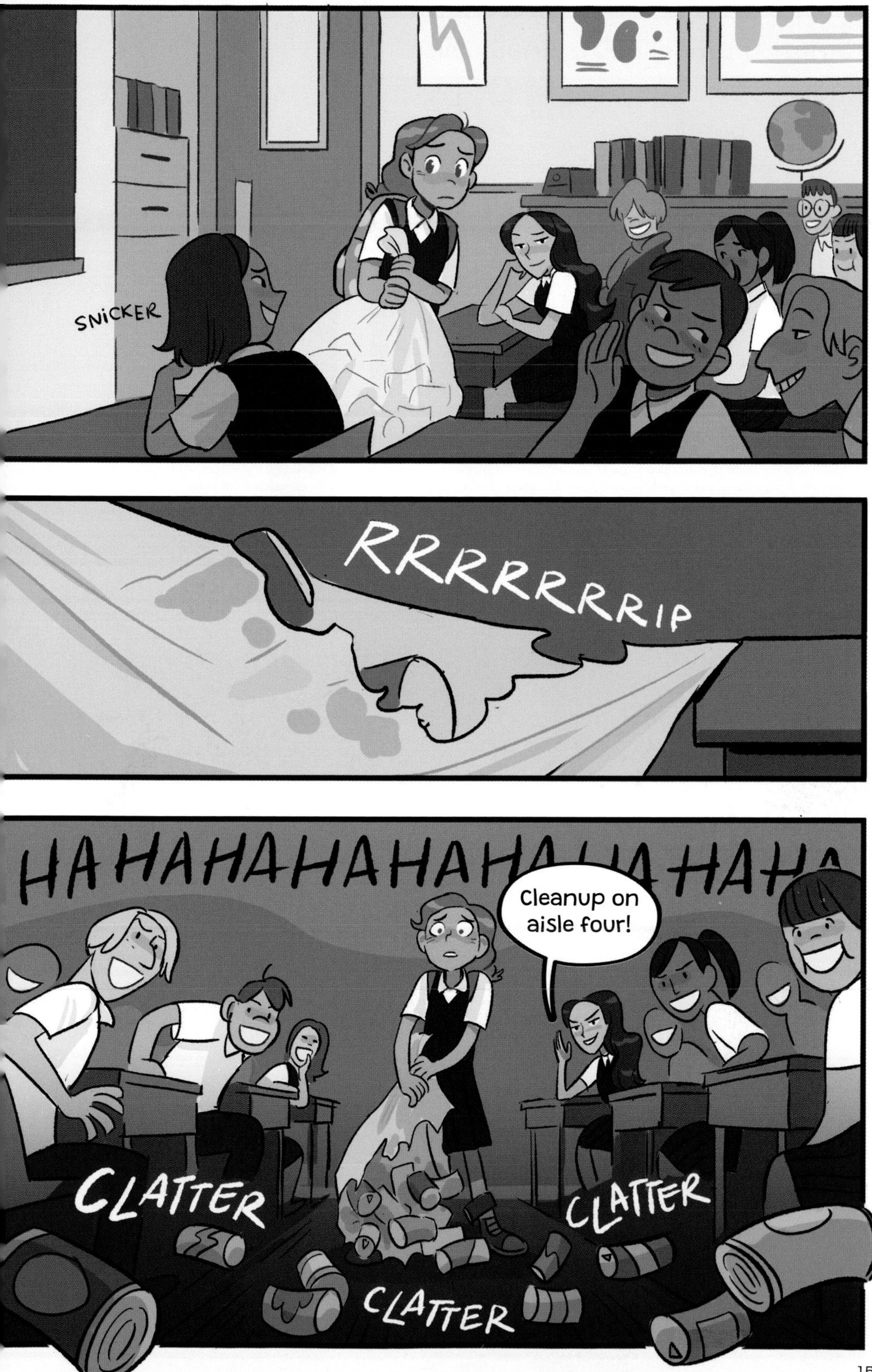
SNICKER
RRRRRRRRIP
HAHAHAHAHAHAHAHAHA
Cleanup on aisle four!
CLATTER
CLATTER
CLATTER

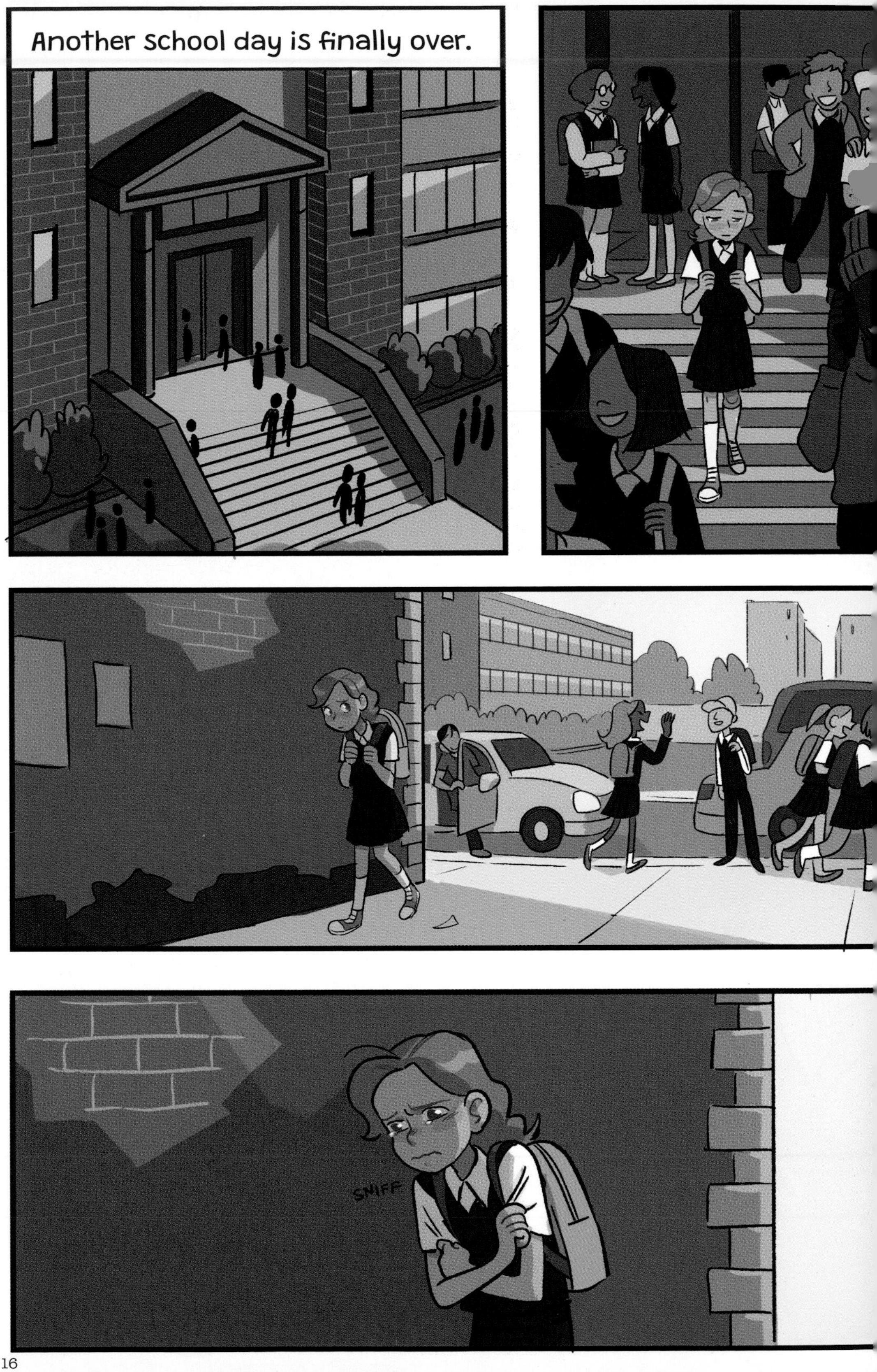
Another school day is finally over.
SNIFF

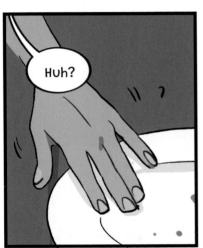

Huh?

You?!

I said "no" to the dog and you *completely* ignored me.

I didn't ignore you—he just showed up. Can't he stay for one night?

Absolutely not! I promised your mom I'd be responsible.

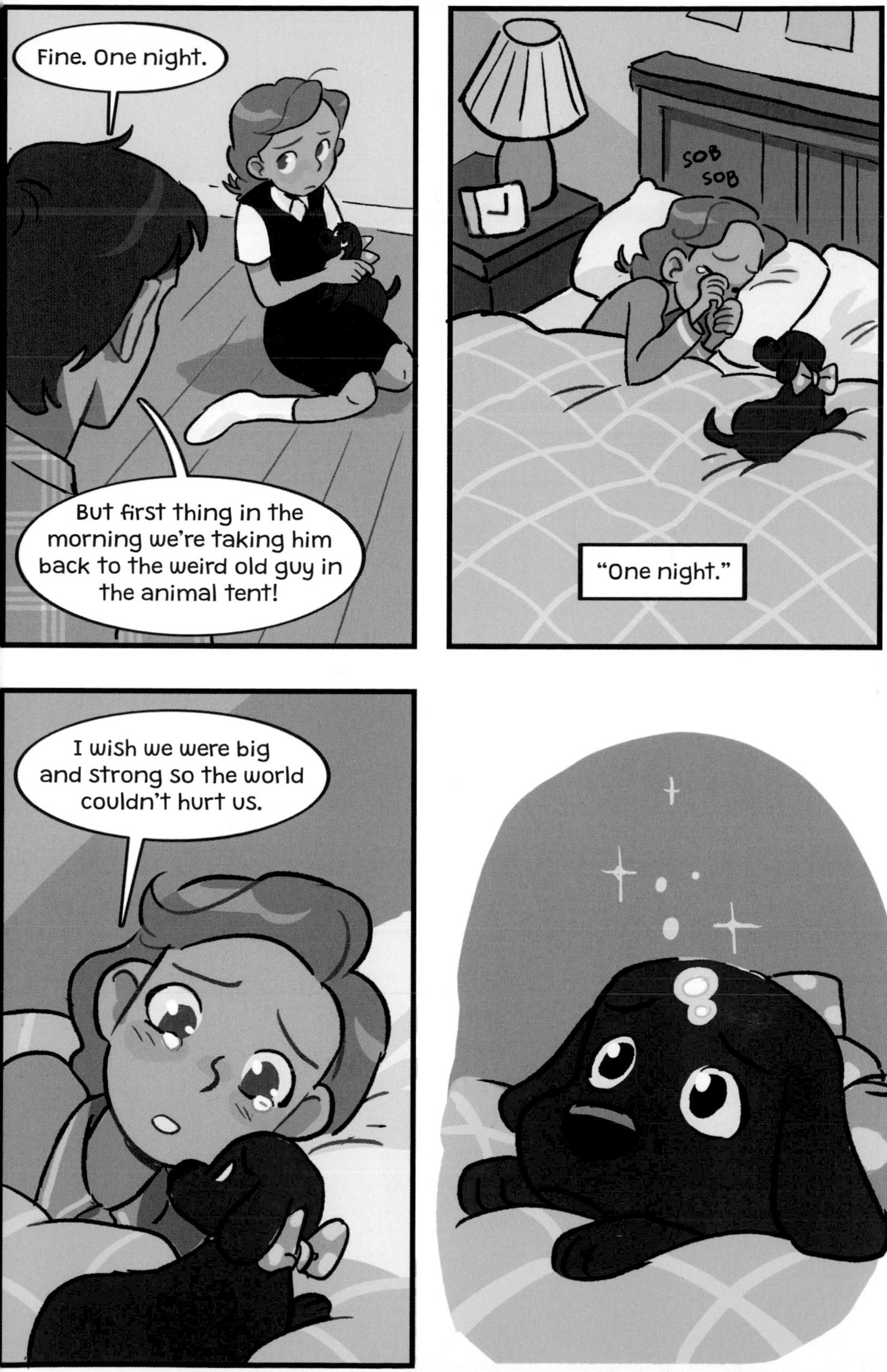
Fine. One night.
But first thing in the morning we're taking him back to the weird old guy in the animal tent!
SOB
SOB
"One night."
I wish we were big and strong so the world couldn't hurt us.

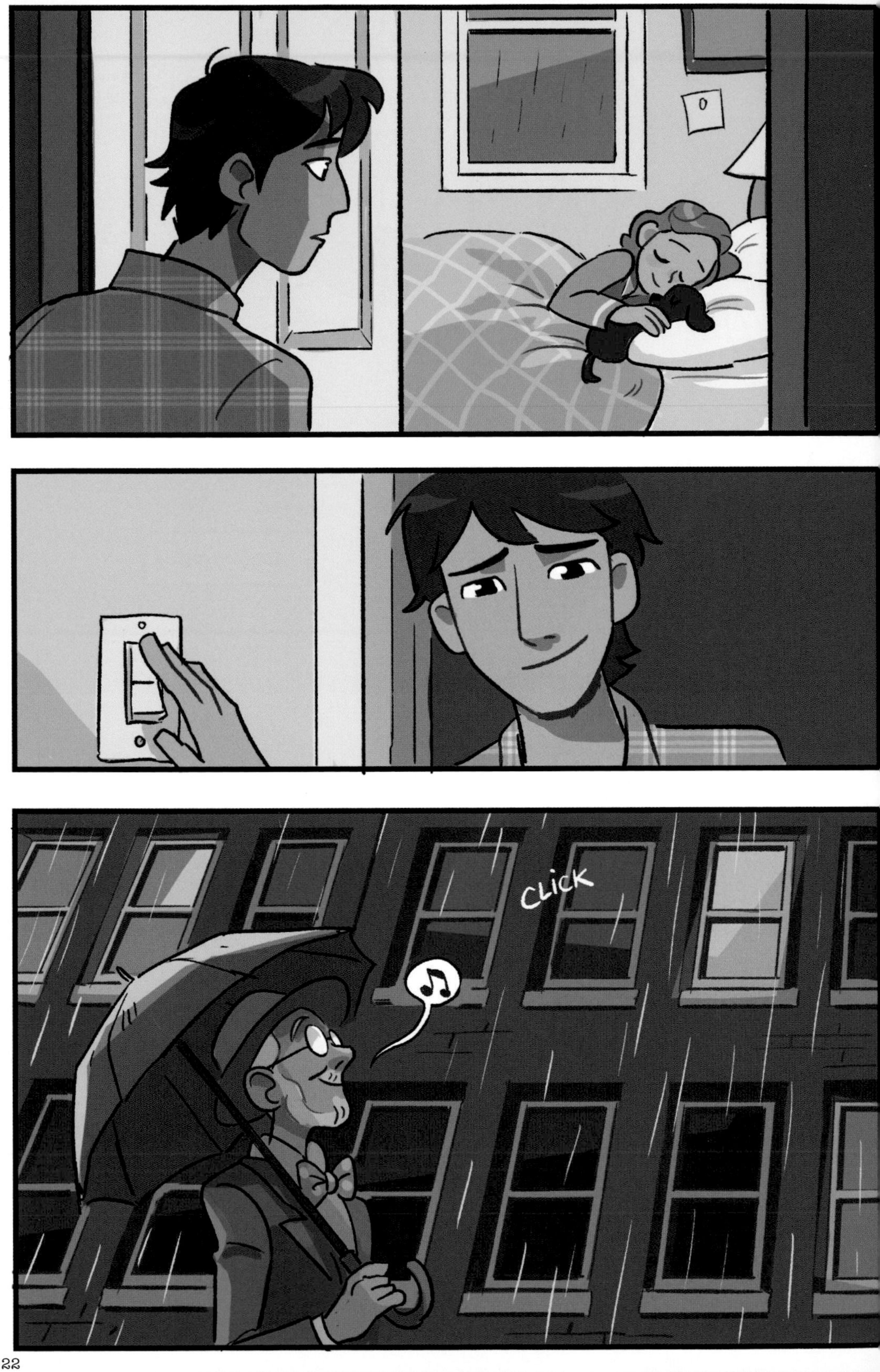
CLICK

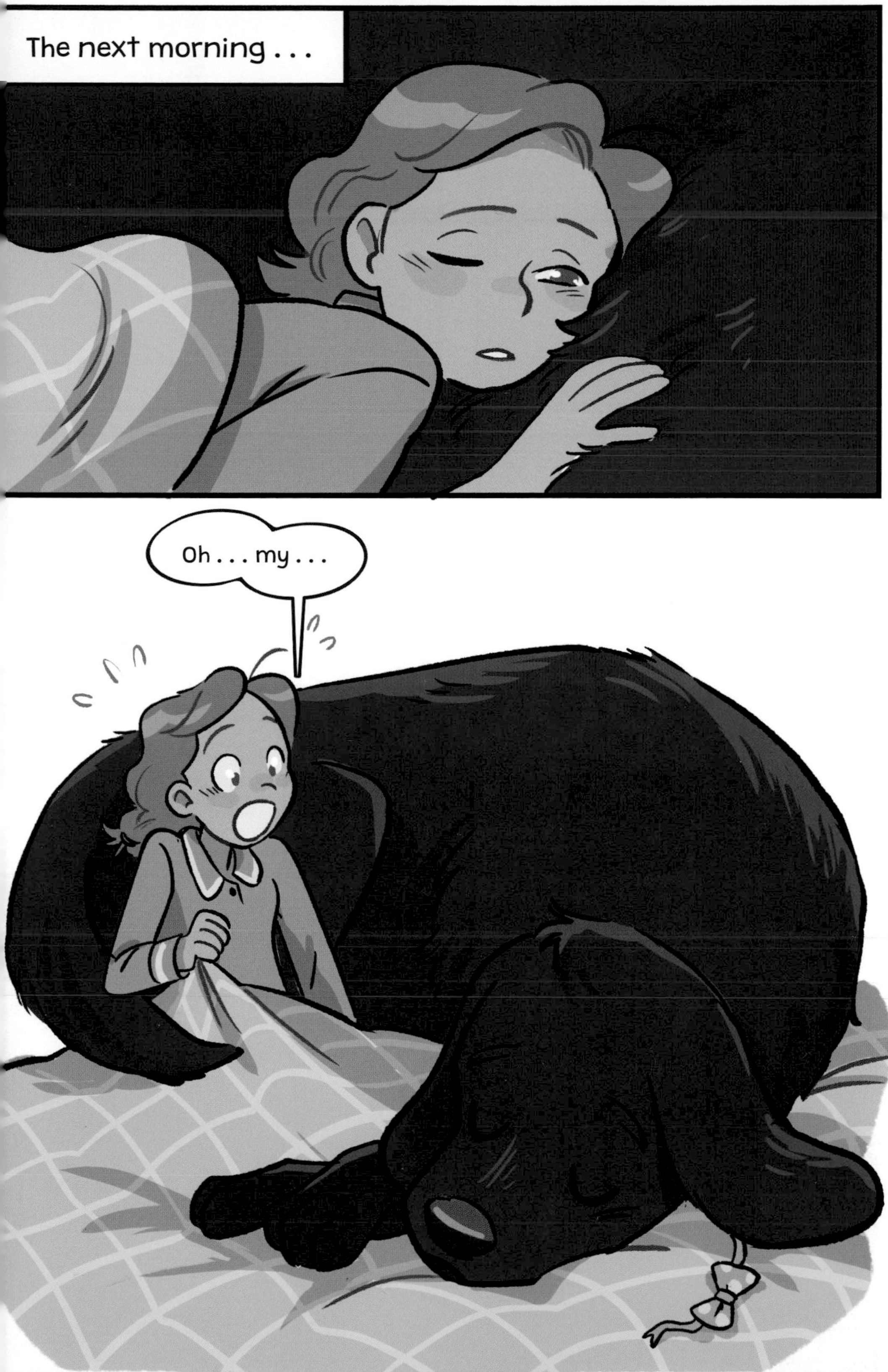
The next morning . . .
Oh . . . my . . .

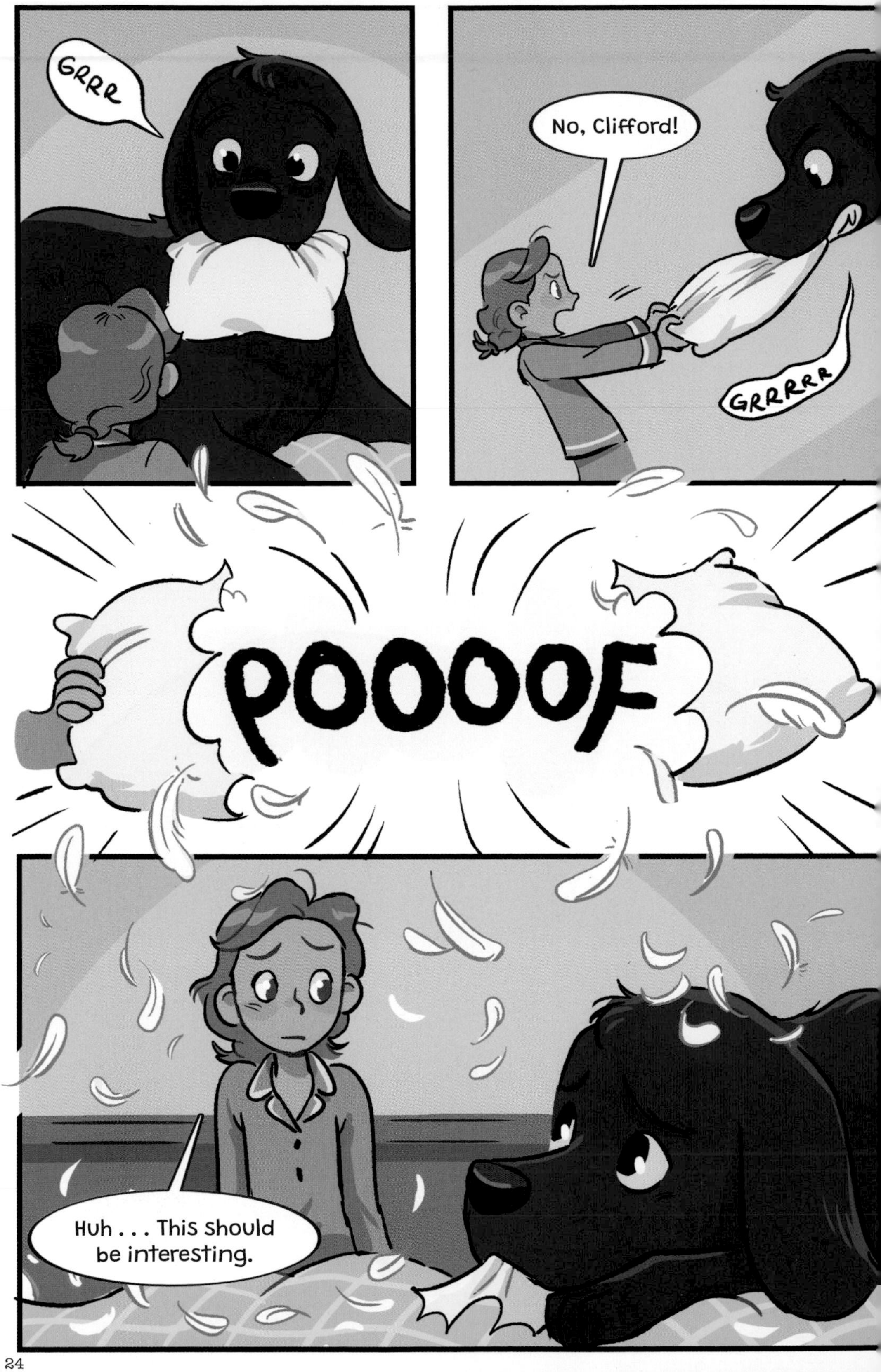
GRRR
No, Clifford!
GRRRRR
POOOOF
Huh . . . This should be interesting.

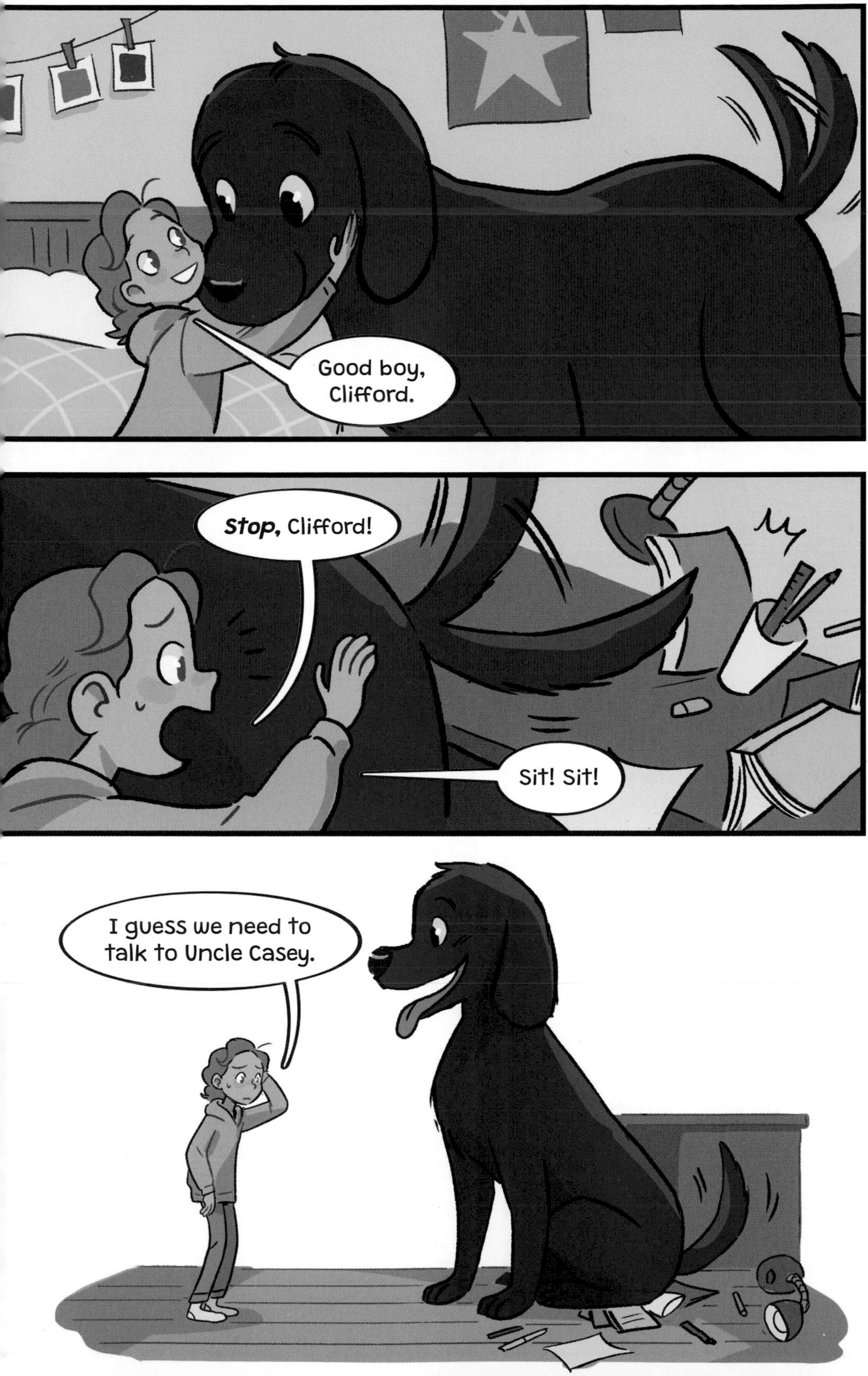
Good boy, Clifford.
Stop, Clifford!
Sit! Sit!
I guess we need to talk to Uncle Casey.

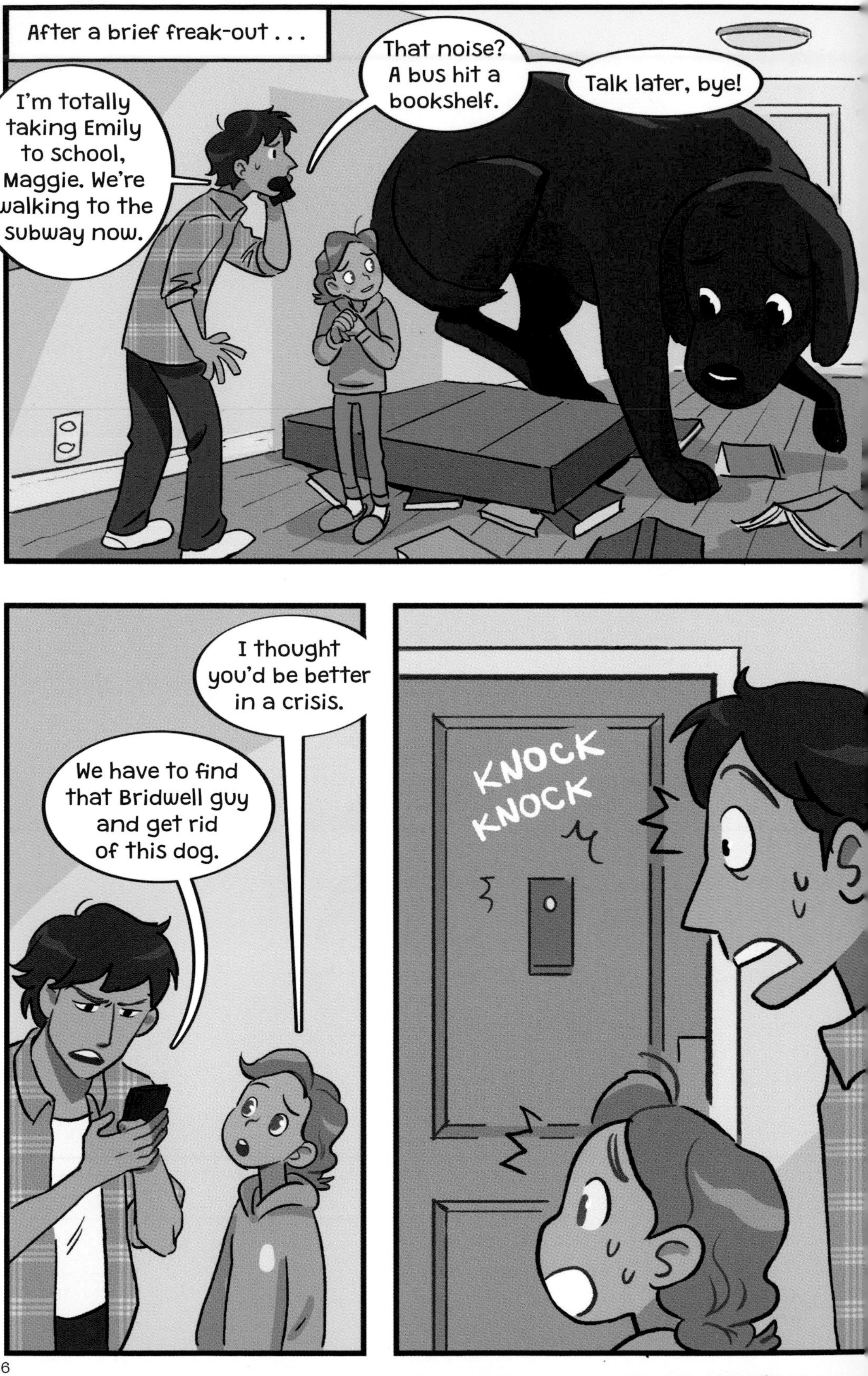
After a brief freak-out . . .
I'm totally taking Emily to school, Maggie. We're walking to the subway now.
That noise? A bus hit a bookshelf.
Talk later, bye!
I thought you'd be better in a crisis.
We have to find that Bridwell guy and get rid of this dog.
KNOCK KNOCK

After their close call with Packard, Casey and Emily take Clifford outside.

How is there no info on this Bridwell guy?

You can't just give people pets that go nuclear and *not* be on the Internet. It's completely irresponsible.

If we can't find Bridwell how are we going to return him?

Return him? No. He needs to see a vet.

A vet?

Yeah! What if he's really sick? There's a vet in that big pet store downtown.

Fine. We'll bring him to a vet.

But after that, we're finding Bridwell and returning his . . . giant dog . . . thing.

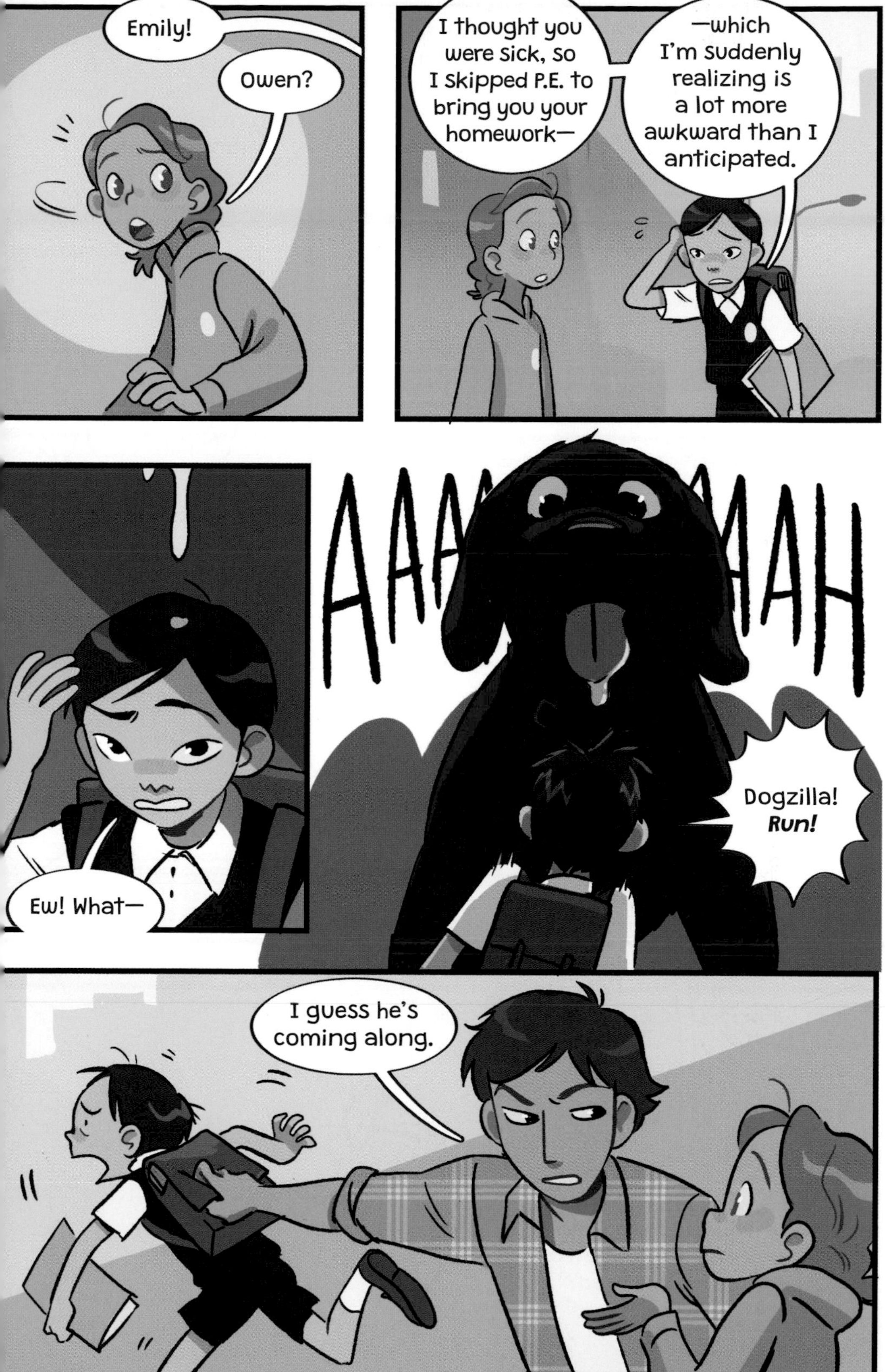
Emily!
Owen?
I thought you were sick, so I skipped P.E. to bring you your homework—
—which I'm suddenly realizing is a lot more awkward than I anticipated.
Ew! What—
AAAAAAAAAAH
Dogzilla! **Run!**
I guess he's coming along.

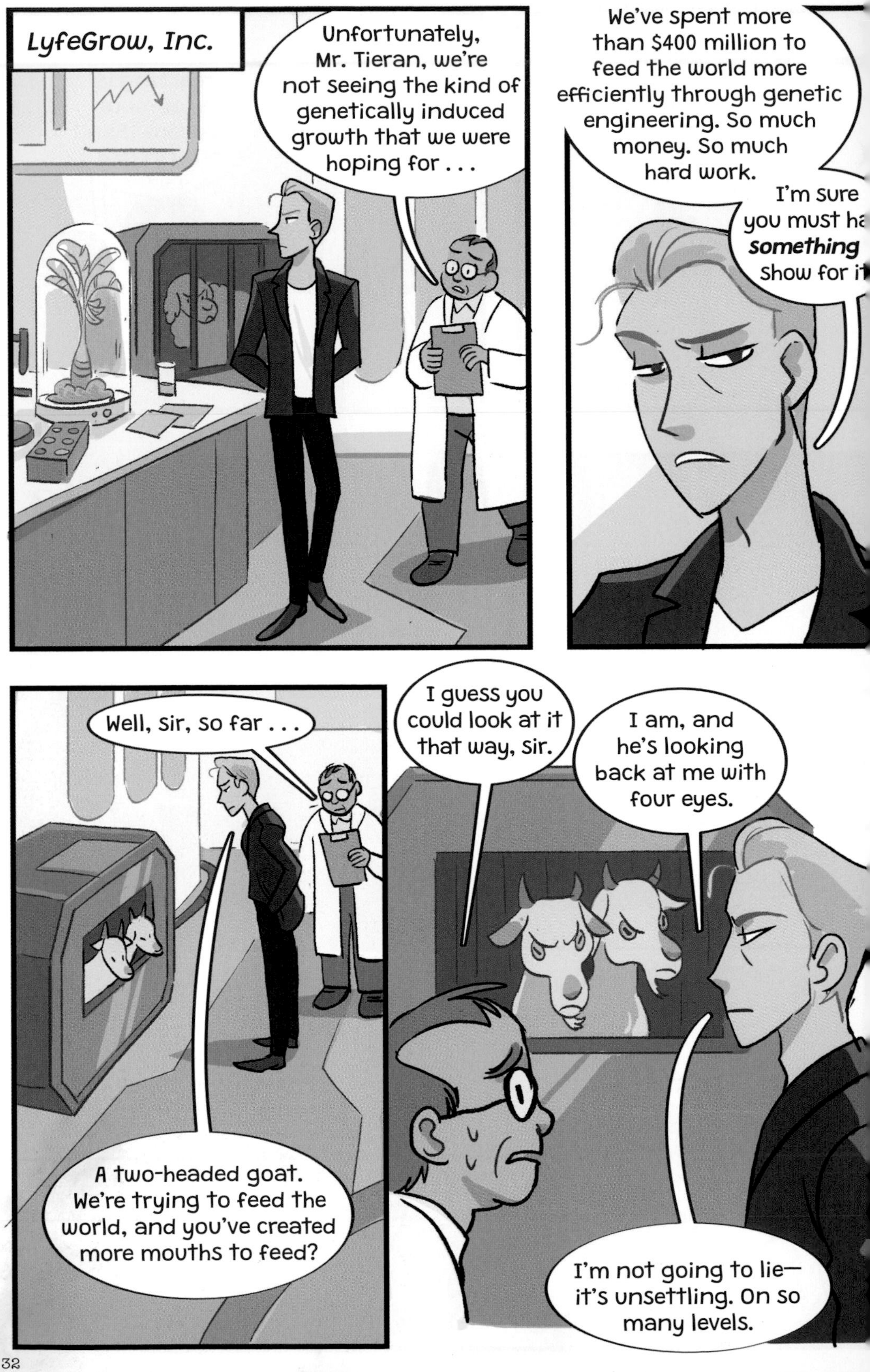
LyfeGrow, Inc.
Unfortunately, Mr. Tieran, we're not seeing the kind of genetically induced growth that we were hoping for . . .
We've spent more than $400 million to feed the world more efficiently through genetic engineering. So much money. So much hard work.
I'm sure you must ha ***something*** show for i
Well, sir, so far . . .
A two-headed goat. We're trying to feed the world, and you've created more mouths to feed?
I guess you could look at it that way, sir.
I am, and he's looking back at me with four eyes.
I'm not going to lie— it's unsettling. On so many levels.

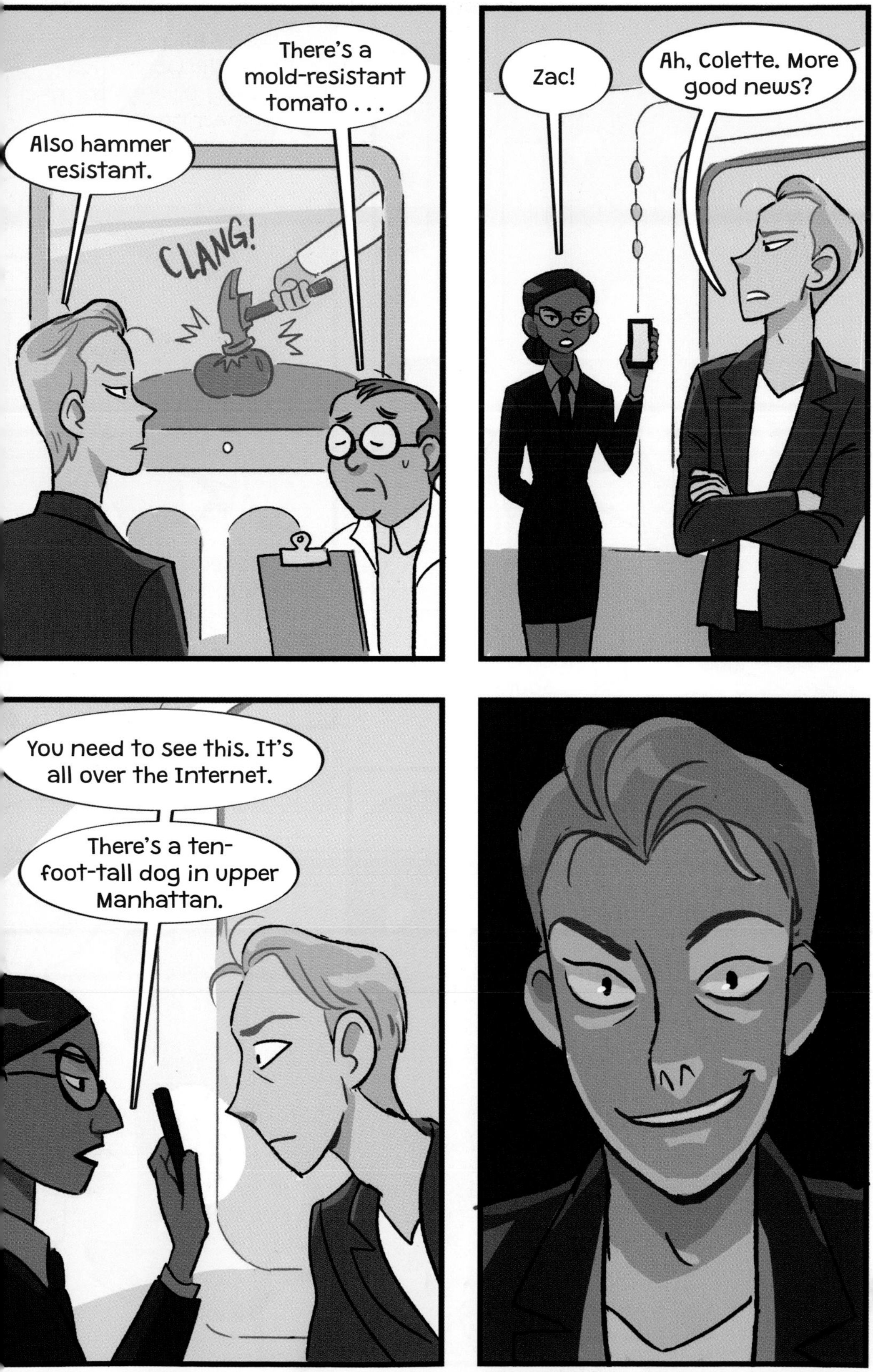
There's a mold-resistant tomato . . .
CLANG!
Also hammer resistant.
Zac!
Ah, Colette. More good news?
You need to see this. It's all over the Internet.
There's a ten-foot-tall dog in upper Manhattan.

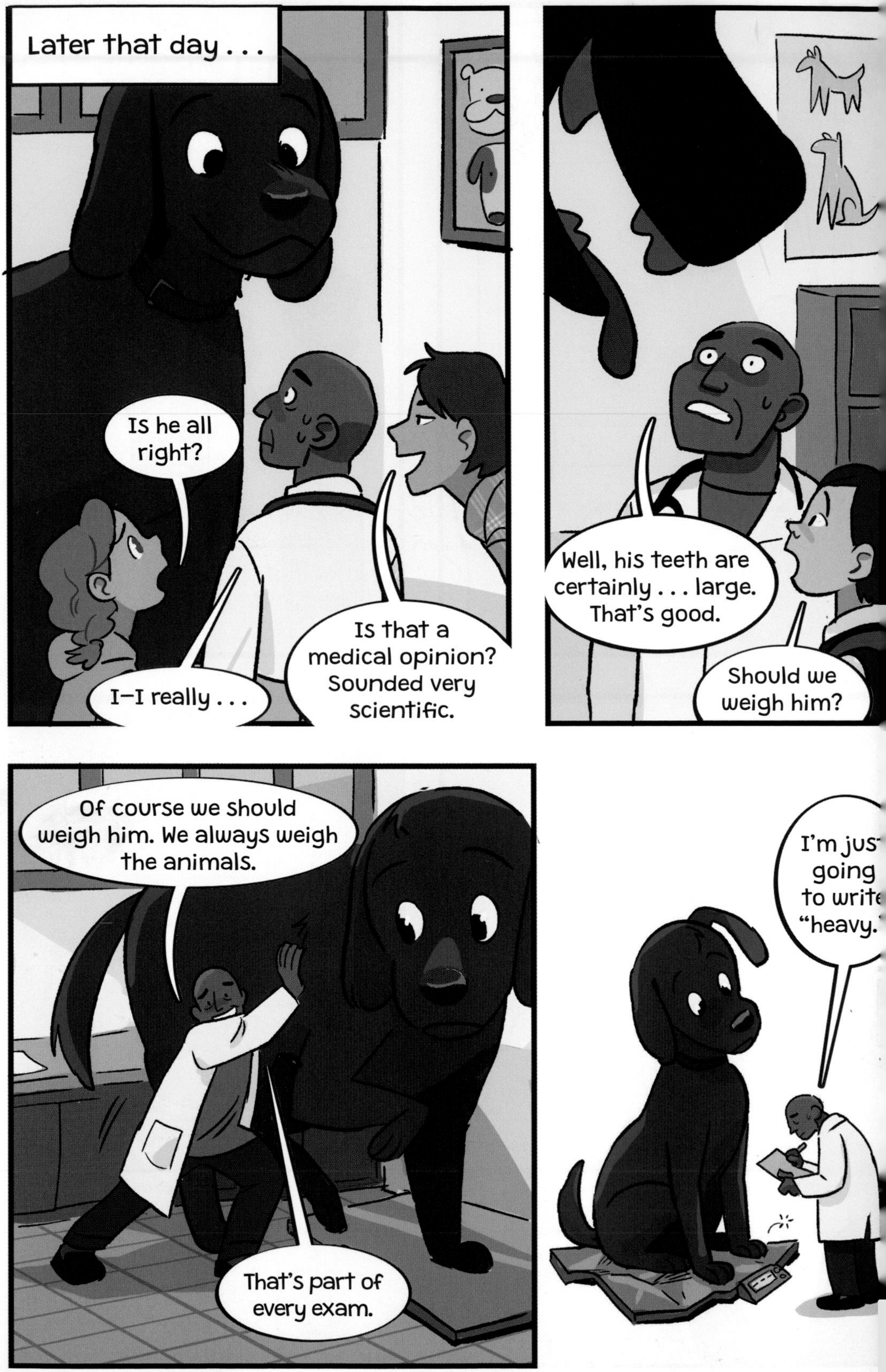
Later that day . . .
Is he all right?
I—I really . . .
Is that a medical opinion? Sounded very scientific.
Well, his teeth are certainly . . . large. That's good.
Should we weigh him?
Of course we should weigh him. We always weigh the animals.
That's part of every exam.
I'm just going to write "heavy."

That's one big handsome fella you got there.

Thank you very much, Lucille.

I meant the dog. Doc says no charge under the circumstances.

You didn't happen to get him from Bridwell, did you?

How did you know?

I've been working in this office for more than twenty years. Whenever someone brings in a "unique" animal, it always seems to come from him.

Bridwell was at our school yesterday. He would have filled out paperwork with his info.

Do you think Bridwell could make Clifford small again??

Are you kidding? That's nothing for a man like Bridwell.

We have to get to the school.

Do you guys have anything that make giant Elmo here any less . . . noticeable?

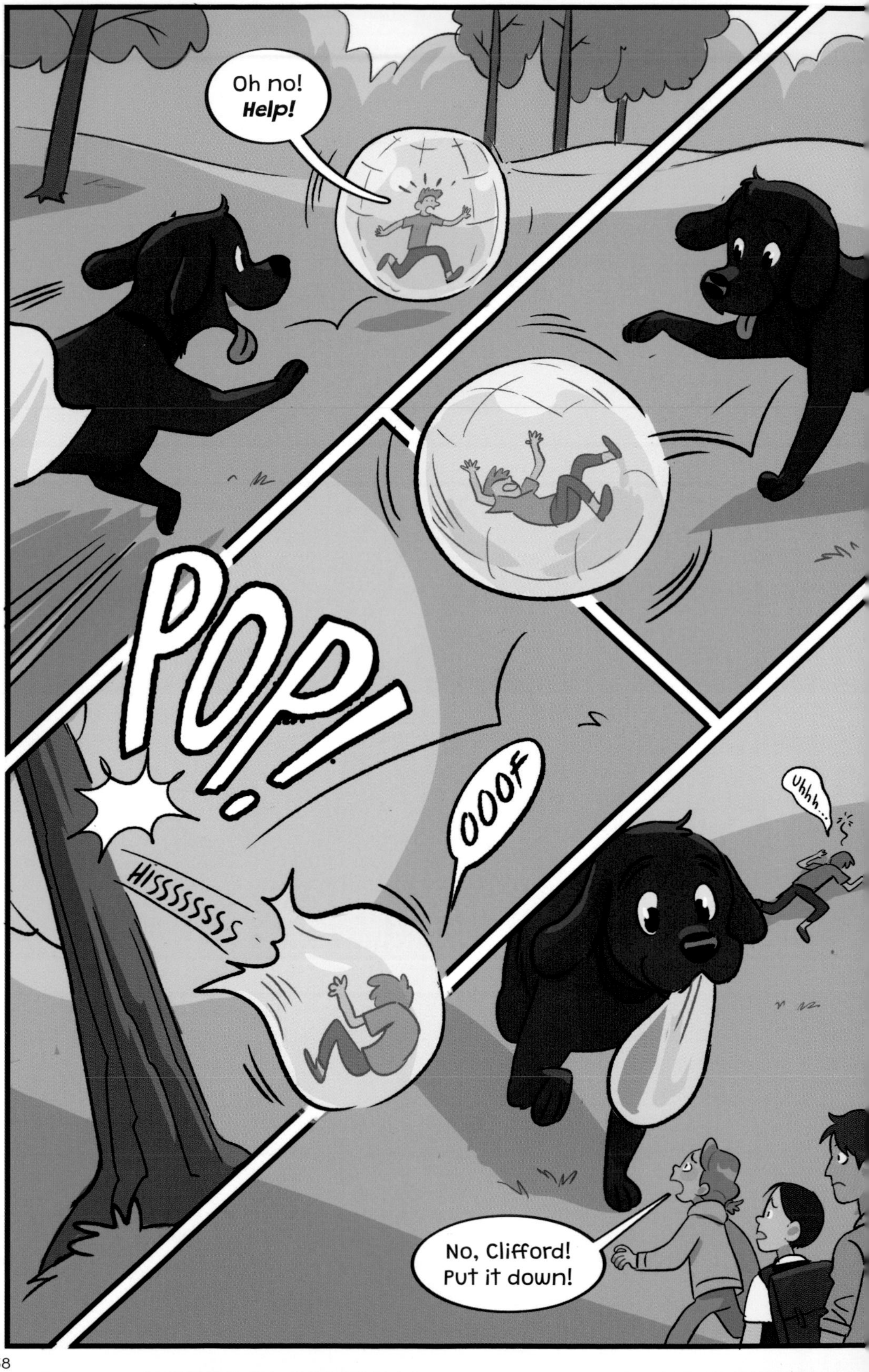
Oh no!
Help!
POP!
HISSSSSSSSS
OOOF
Uhhh...
No, Clifford!
Put it down!

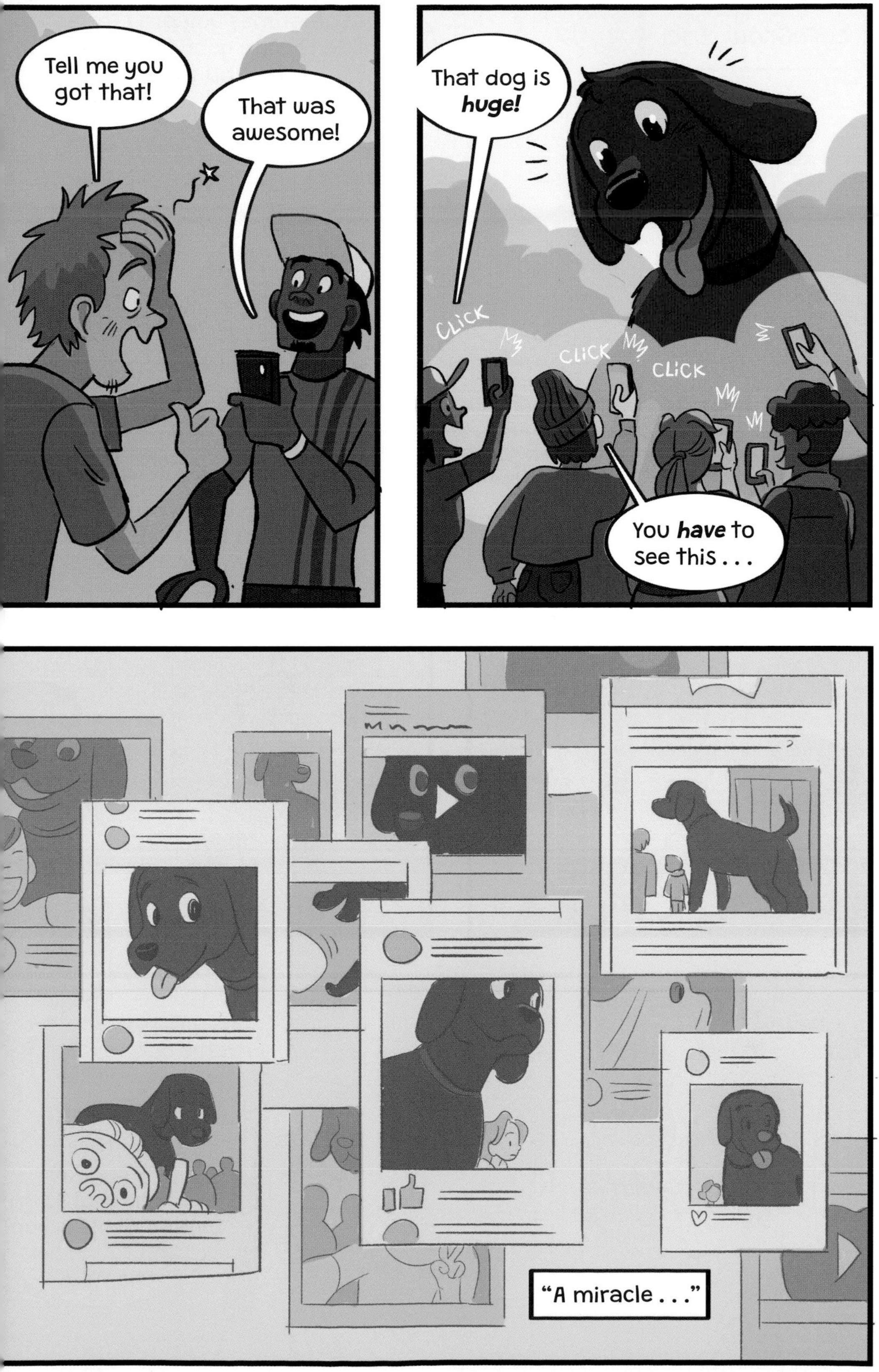
Tell me you got that!
That was awesome!
That dog is *huge!*
CLICK
CLICK
CLICK
You *have* to see this . . .
"A miracle . . ."

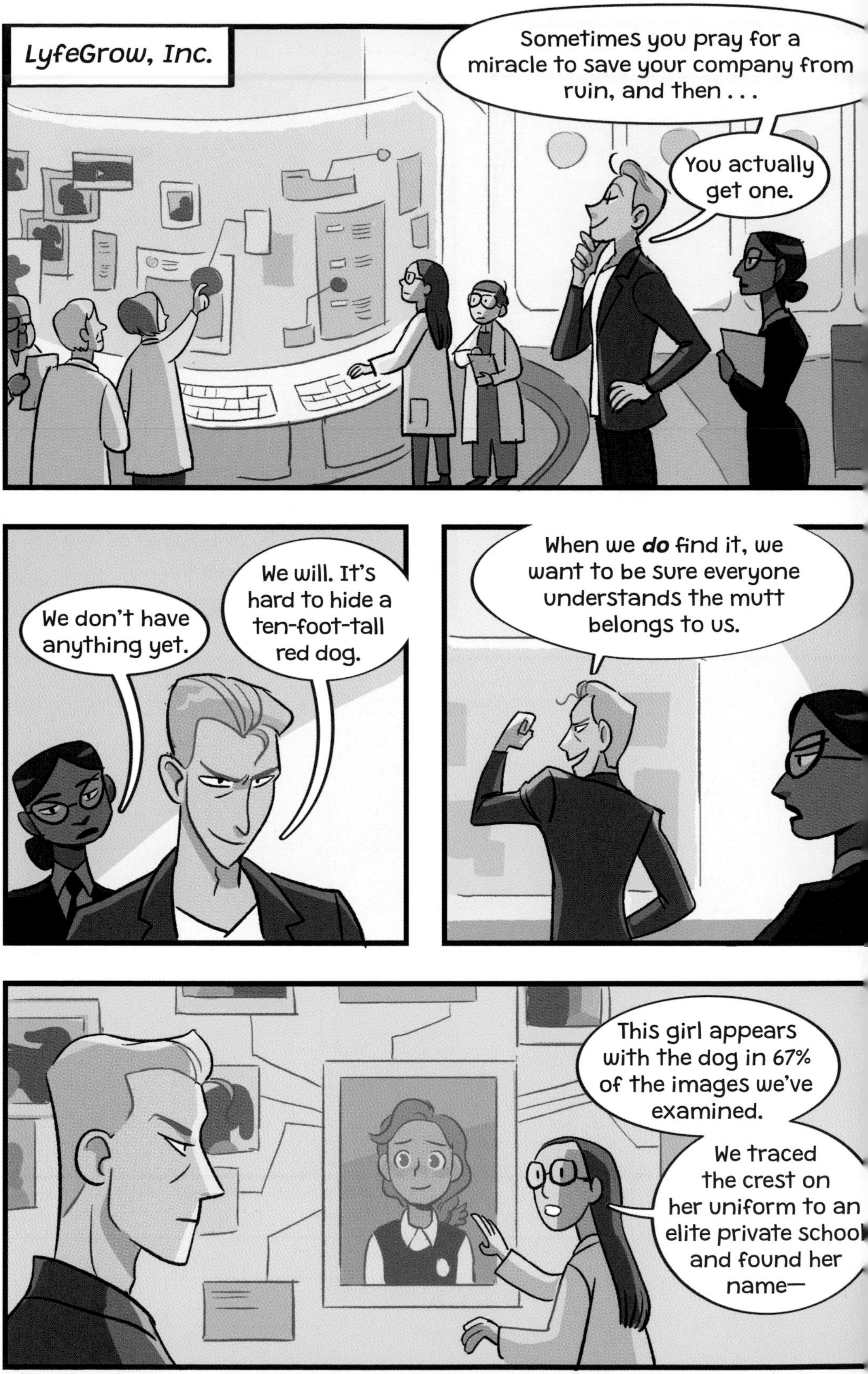
LyfeGrow, Inc.
Sometimes you pray for a miracle to save your company from ruin, and then . . .
You actually get one.
We don't have anything yet.
We will. It's hard to hide a ten-foot-tall red dog.
When we *do* find it, we want to be sure everyone understands the mutt belongs to us.
This girl appears with the dog in 67% of the images we've examined.
We traced the crest on her uniform to an elite private school and found her name—

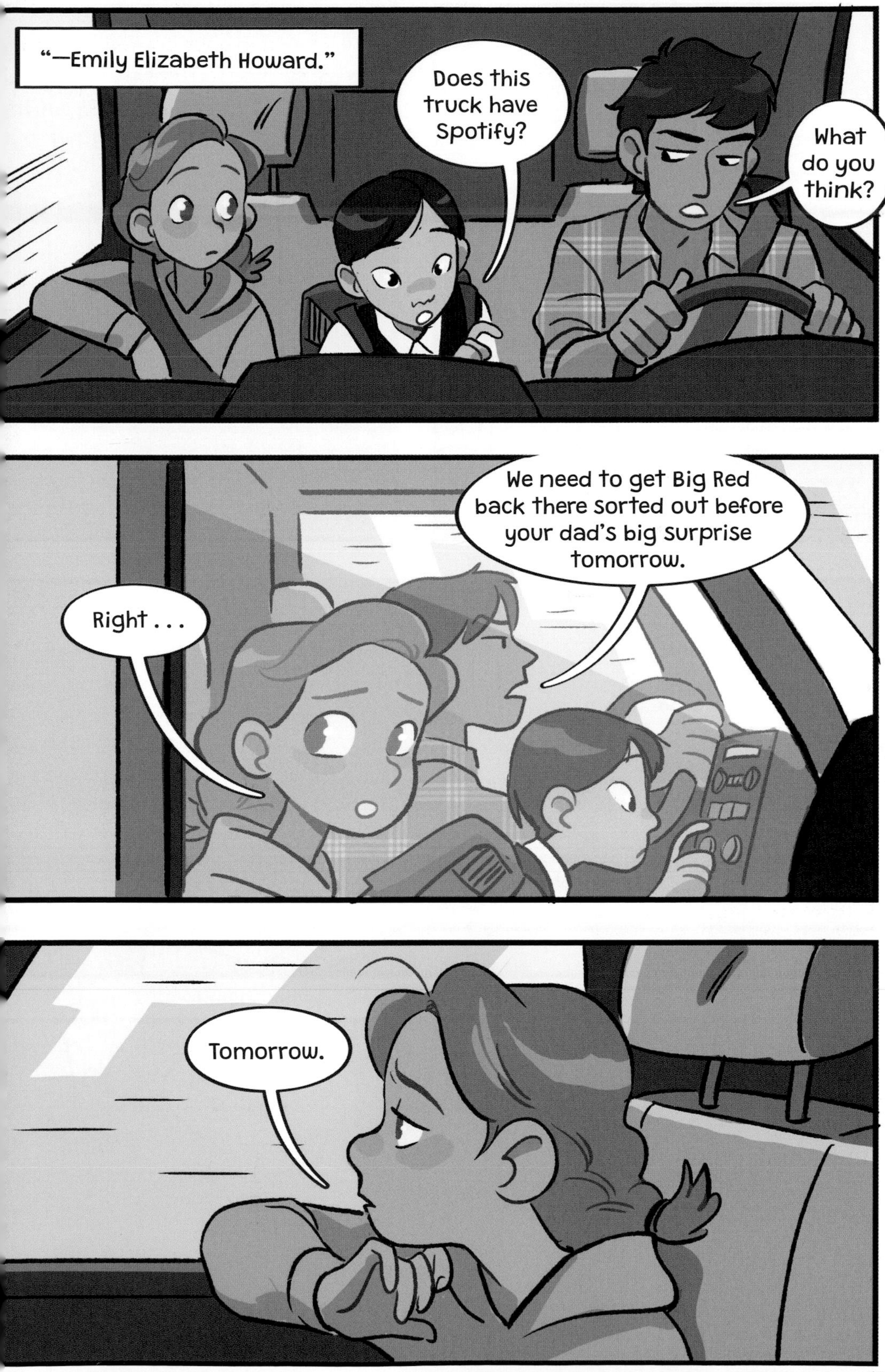
"—Emily Elizabeth Howard."
Does this truck have Spotify?
What do you think?
We need to get Big Red back there sorted out before your dad's big surprise tomorrow.
Right . . .
Tomorrow.

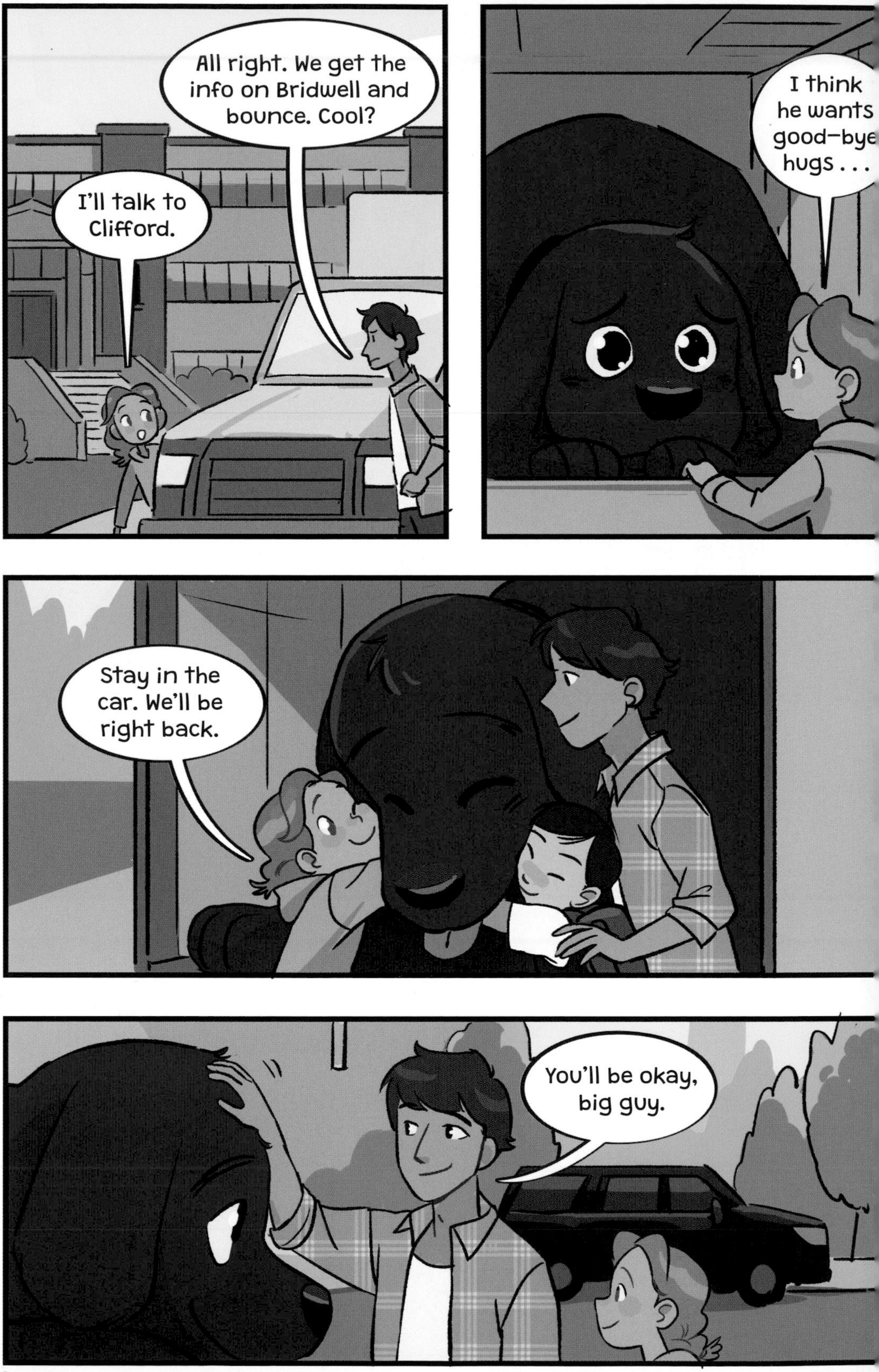
I'll talk to Clifford.
All right. We get the info on Bridwell and bounce. Cool?
I think he wants good-bye hugs . . .
Stay in the car. We'll be right back.
You'll be okay, big guy.

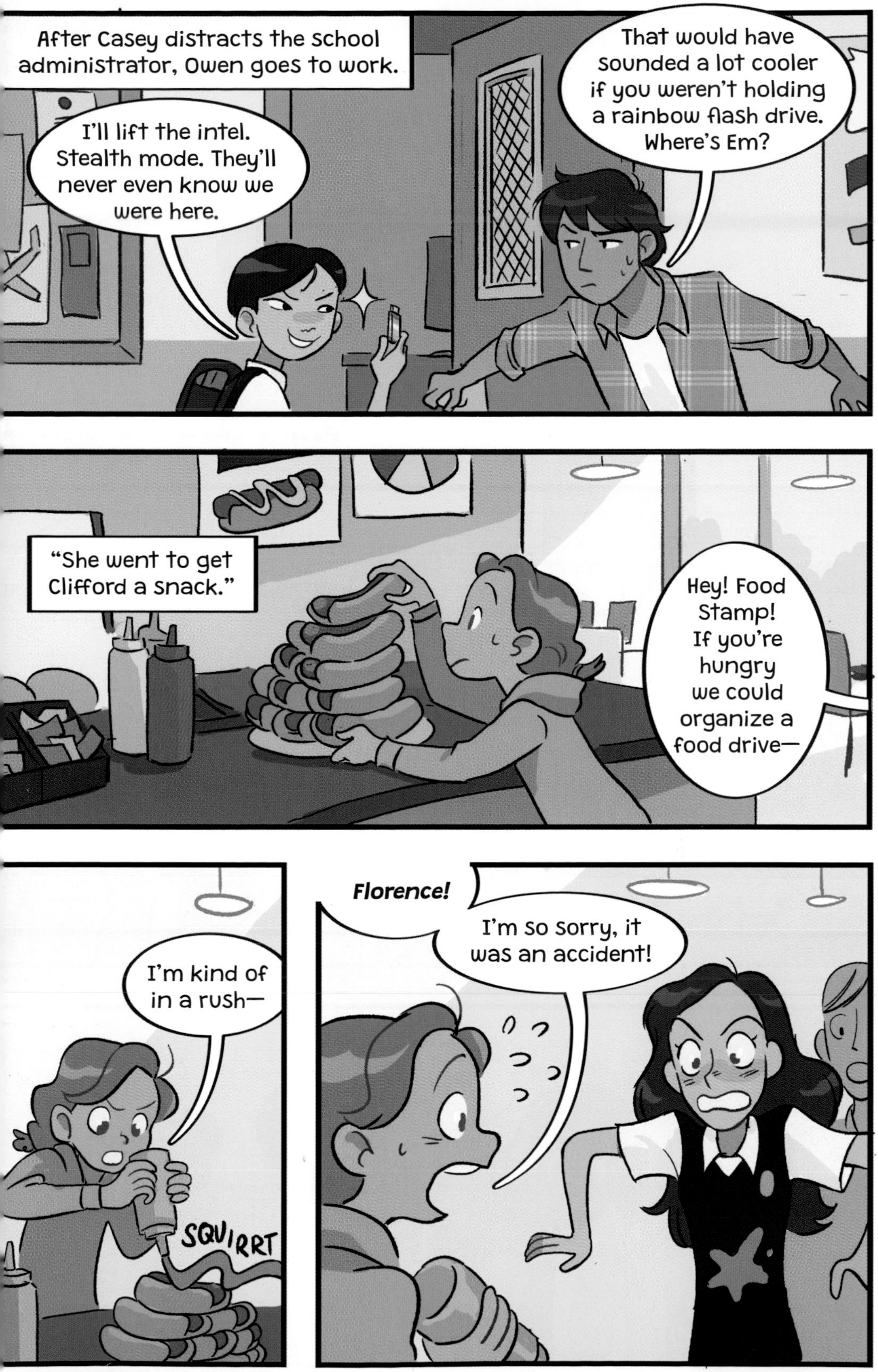
After Casey distracts the school administrator, Owen goes to work.
I'll lift the intel. Stealth mode. They'll never even know we were here.
That would have sounded a lot cooler if you weren't holding a rainbow flash drive. Where's Em?
"She went to get Clifford a snack."
Hey! Food Stamp! If you're hungry we could organize a food drive—
I'm kind of in a rush—
SQUIRRT
Florence!
I'm so sorry, it was an accident!

44

Back at Emily's apartment . . .

Standing up to Florence felt really good.

The Wicked Witch is dead!

Focus! After we download the info on Bridwell we need to—

Wait— Packard . . . is evicting us?!

EVICTION NOTICE

I KNEW I Smelled DOG!

This can't be happening . . .

Someone must have sent Packard those pictures of Clifford.

What am I going to say the next time your mother calls?

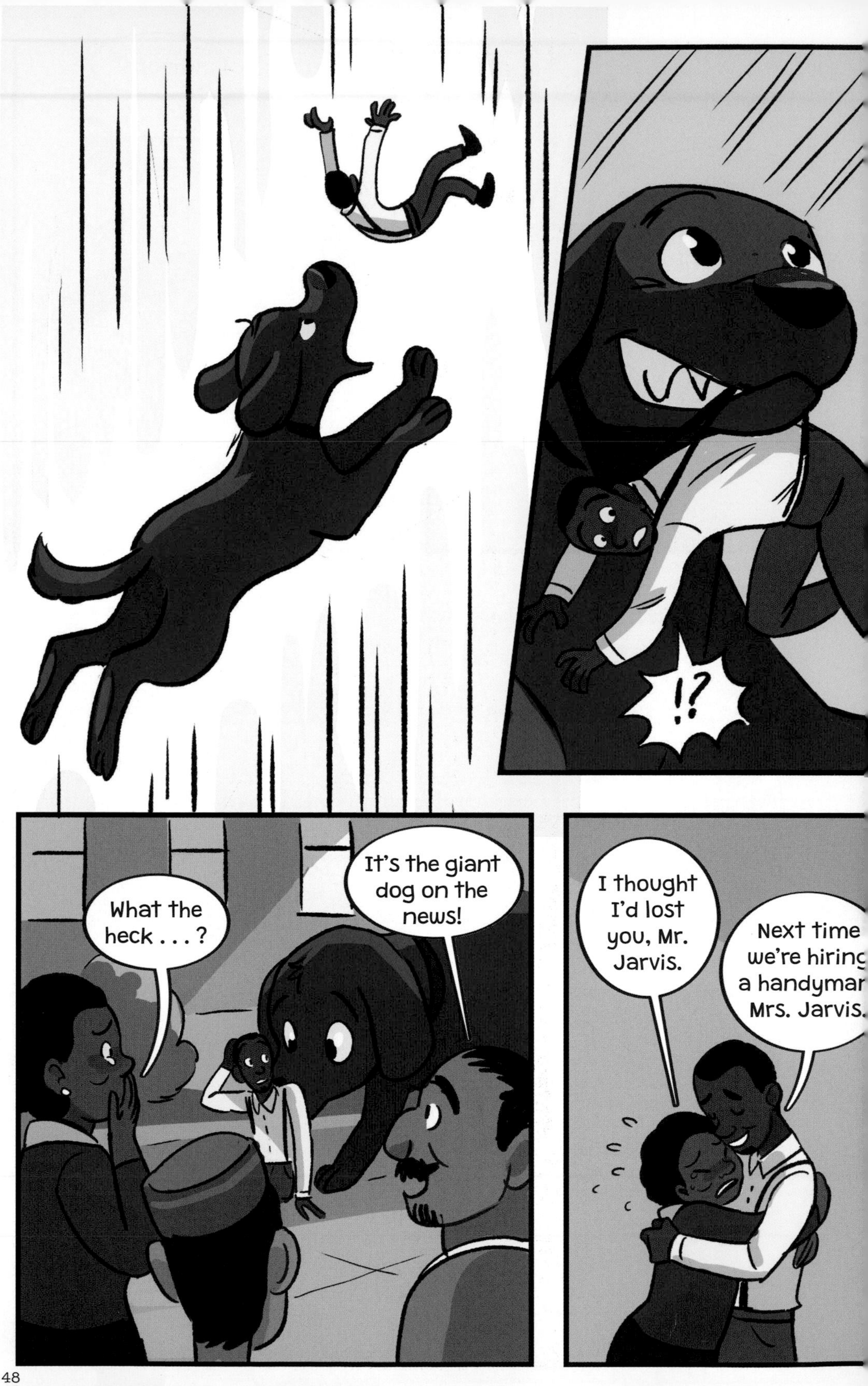
!?
What the heck . . . ?
It's the giant dog on the news!
I thought I'd lost you, Mr. Jarvis.
Next time we're hiring a handyman, Mrs. Jarvis.

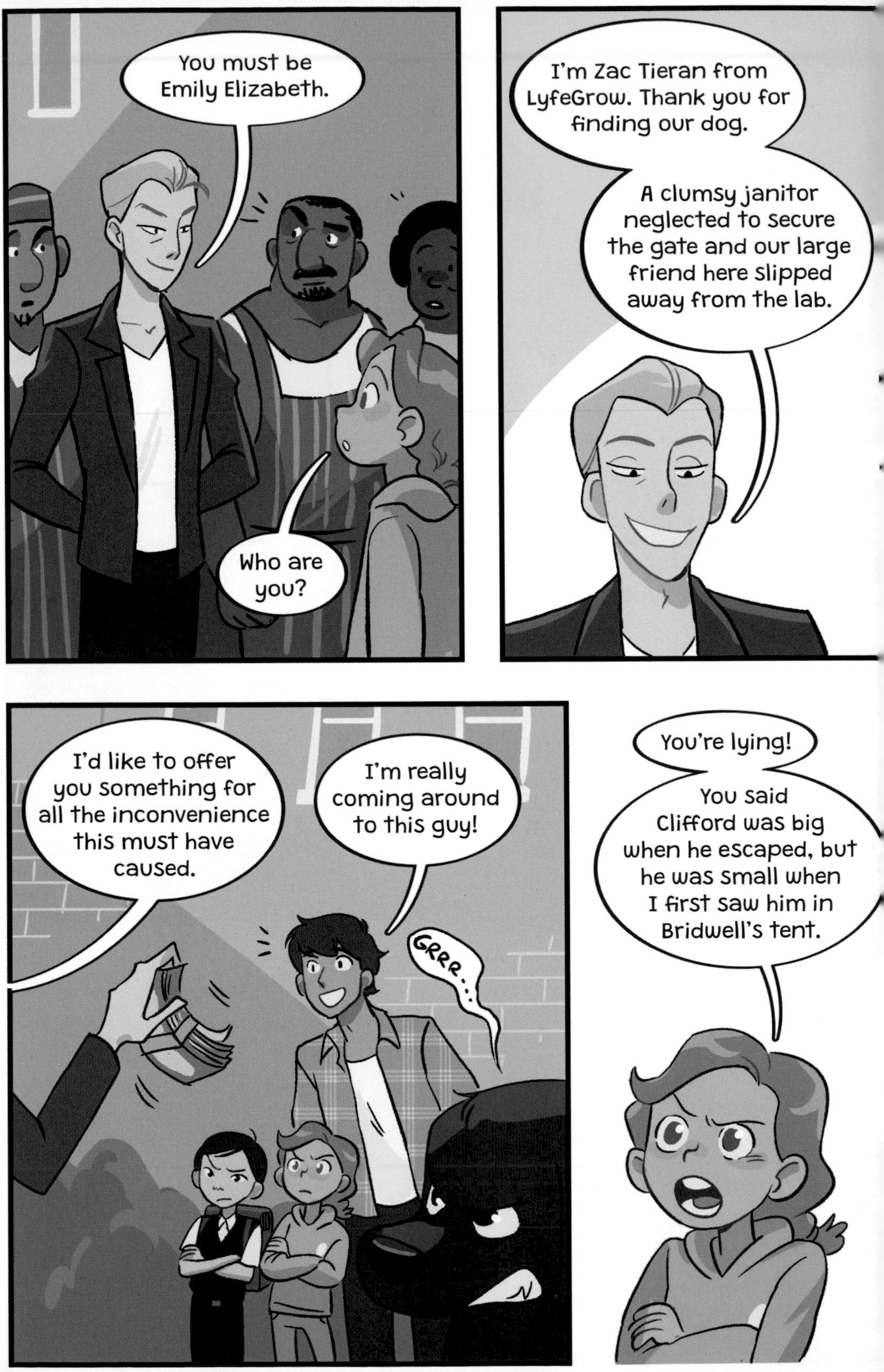
You must be Emily Elizabeth.
Who are you?
I'm Zac Tieran from LyfeGrow. Thank you for finding our dog.
A clumsy janitor neglected to secure the gate and our large friend here slipped away from the lab.
I'd like to offer you something for all the inconvenience this must have caused.
I'm really coming around to this guy!
GRRR...
You're lying!
You said Clifford was big when he escaped, but he was small when I first saw him in Bridwell's tent.

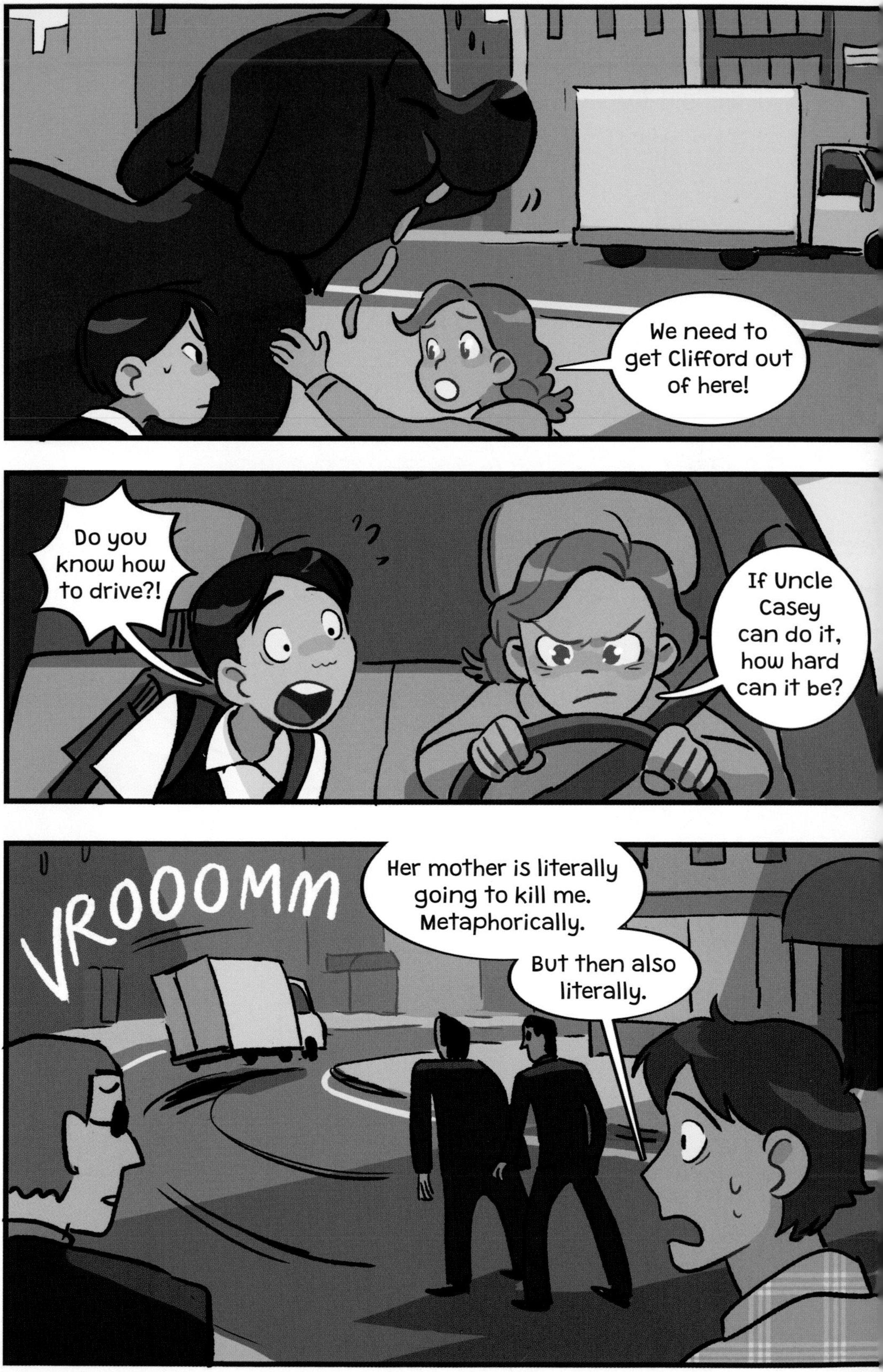
We need to get Clifford out of here!
Do you know how to drive?!
If Uncle Casey can do it, how hard can it be?
VROOOMM
Her mother is literally going to kill me. Metaphorically.
But then also literally.

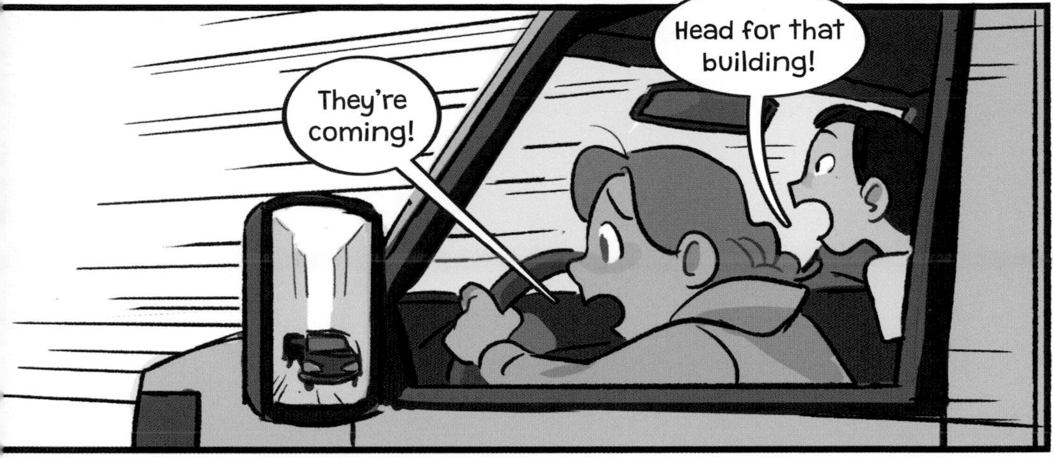
They're coming!
Head for that building!

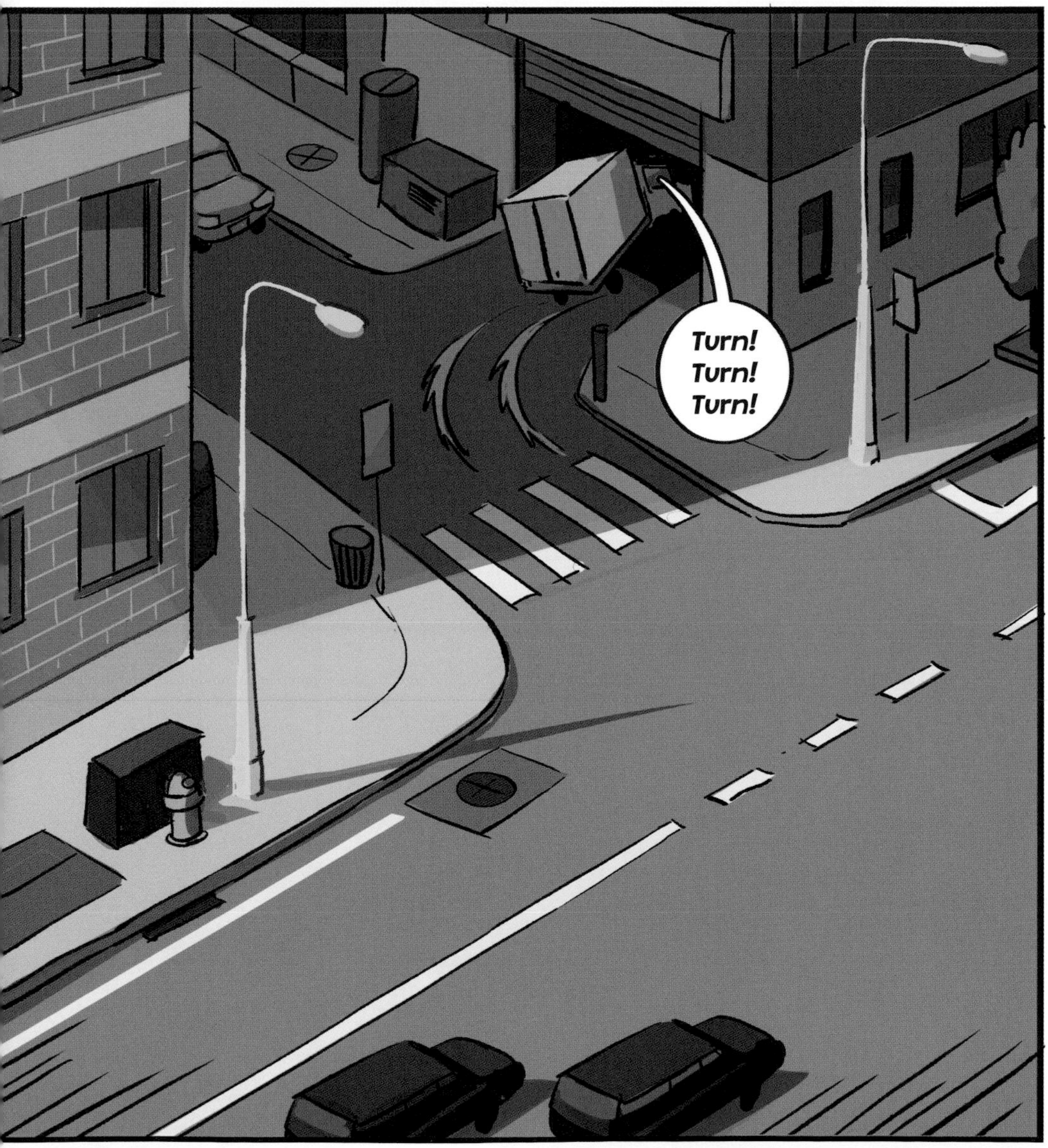
Turn! Turn! Turn!

Your mother is going to find out the truth sooner or later.

Especially after your dad shows up at a padlocked apartment.

My dad's not coming tomorrow . . .

CLICK

What about the big surprise weekend?

That wasn't for me. It was for his new family. He's got a girlfriend.

With kids.

Oh, Em. I'm sorry.

Guys, look at this.

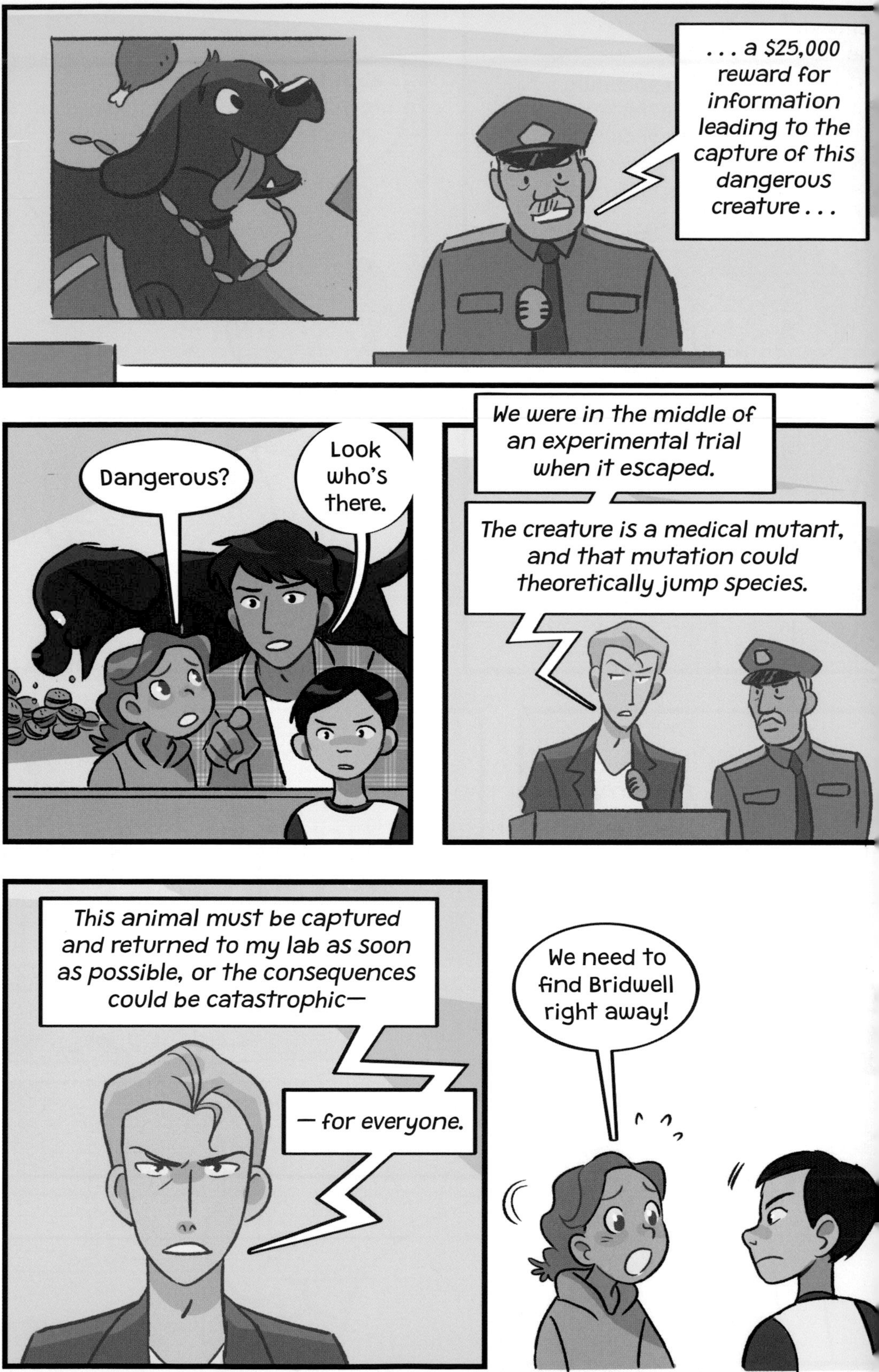
. . . a $25,000 reward for information leading to the capture of this dangerous creature . . .
Dangerous?
Look who's there.
We were in the middle of an experimental trial when it escaped.
The creature is a medical mutant, and that mutation could theoretically jump species.
This animal must be captured and returned to my lab as soon as possible, or the consequences could be catastrophic—
— for everyone.
We need to find Bridwell right away!

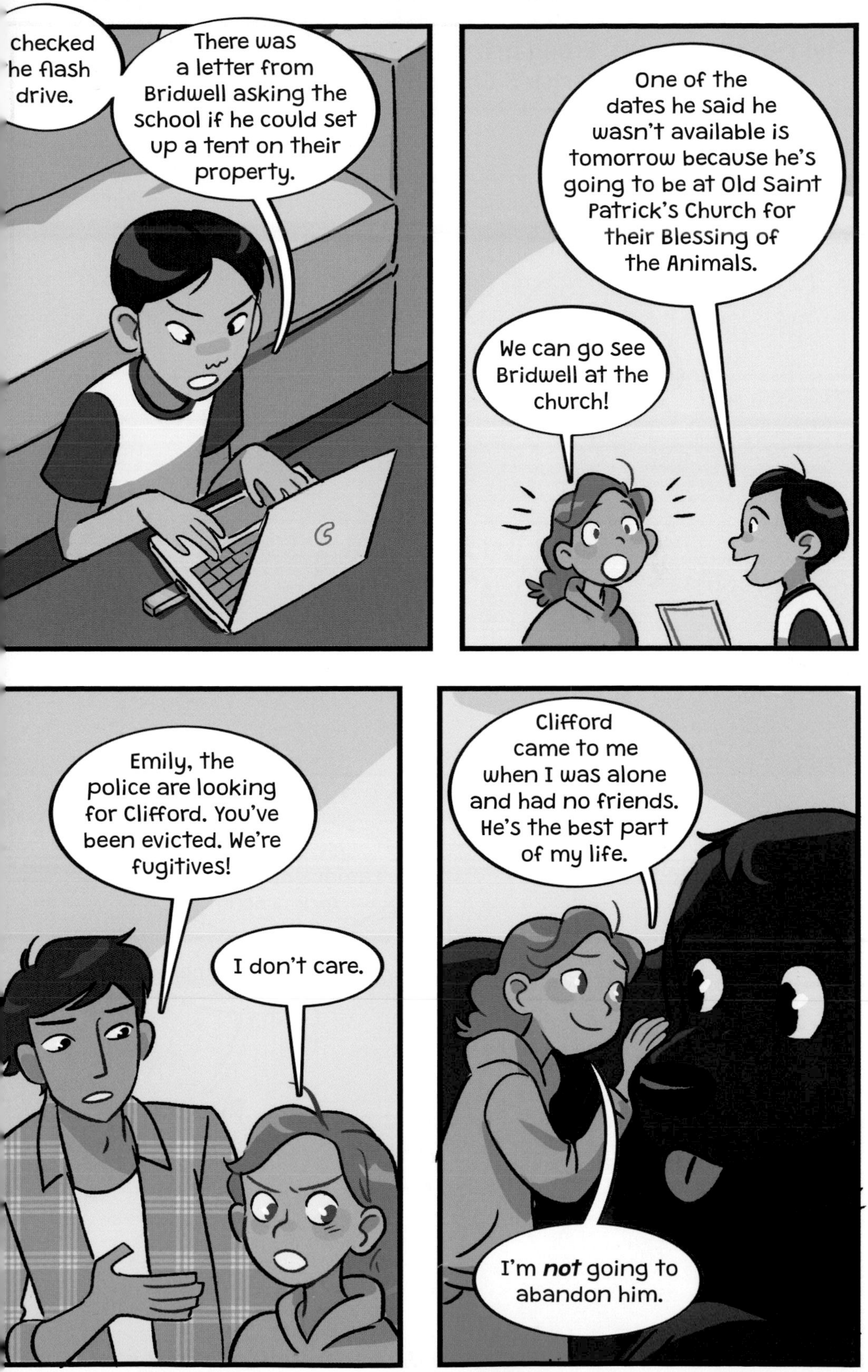
checked
he flash
drive.
There was a letter from Bridwell asking the school if he could set up a tent on their property.
One of the dates he said he wasn't available is tomorrow because he's going to be at Old Saint Patrick's Church for their Blessing of the Animals.
We can go see Bridwell at the church!
Emily, the police are looking for Clifford. You've been evicted. We're fugitives!
I don't care.
Clifford came to me when I was alone and had no friends. He's the best part of my life.
I'm ***not*** going to abandon him.

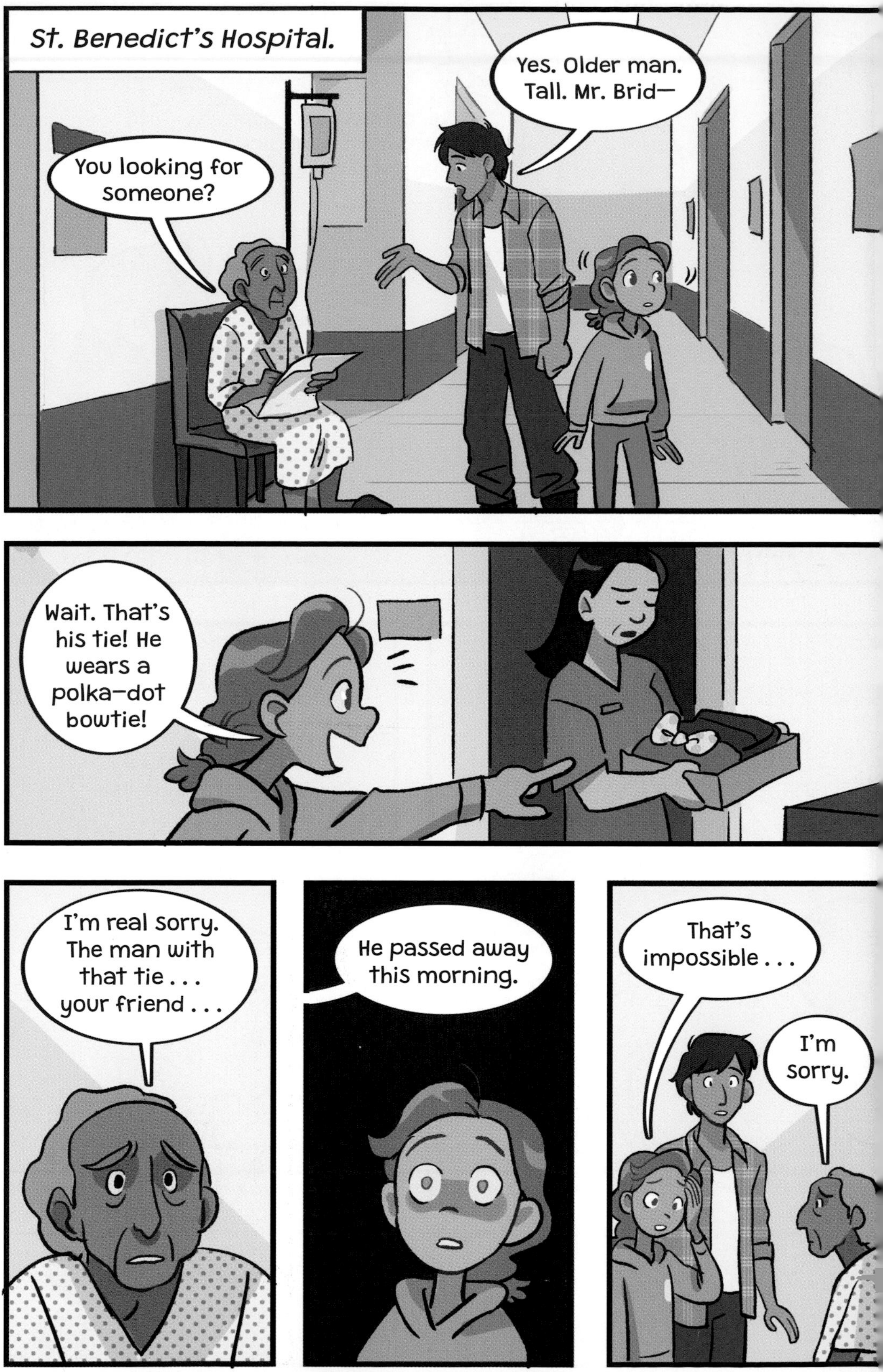
St. Benedict's Hospital.
You looking for someone?
Yes. Older man. Tall. Mr. Brid—
Wait. That's his tie! He wears a polka-dot bowtie!
I'm real sorry. The man with that tie . . . your friend . . .
He passed away this morning.
That's impossible . . .
I'm sorry.

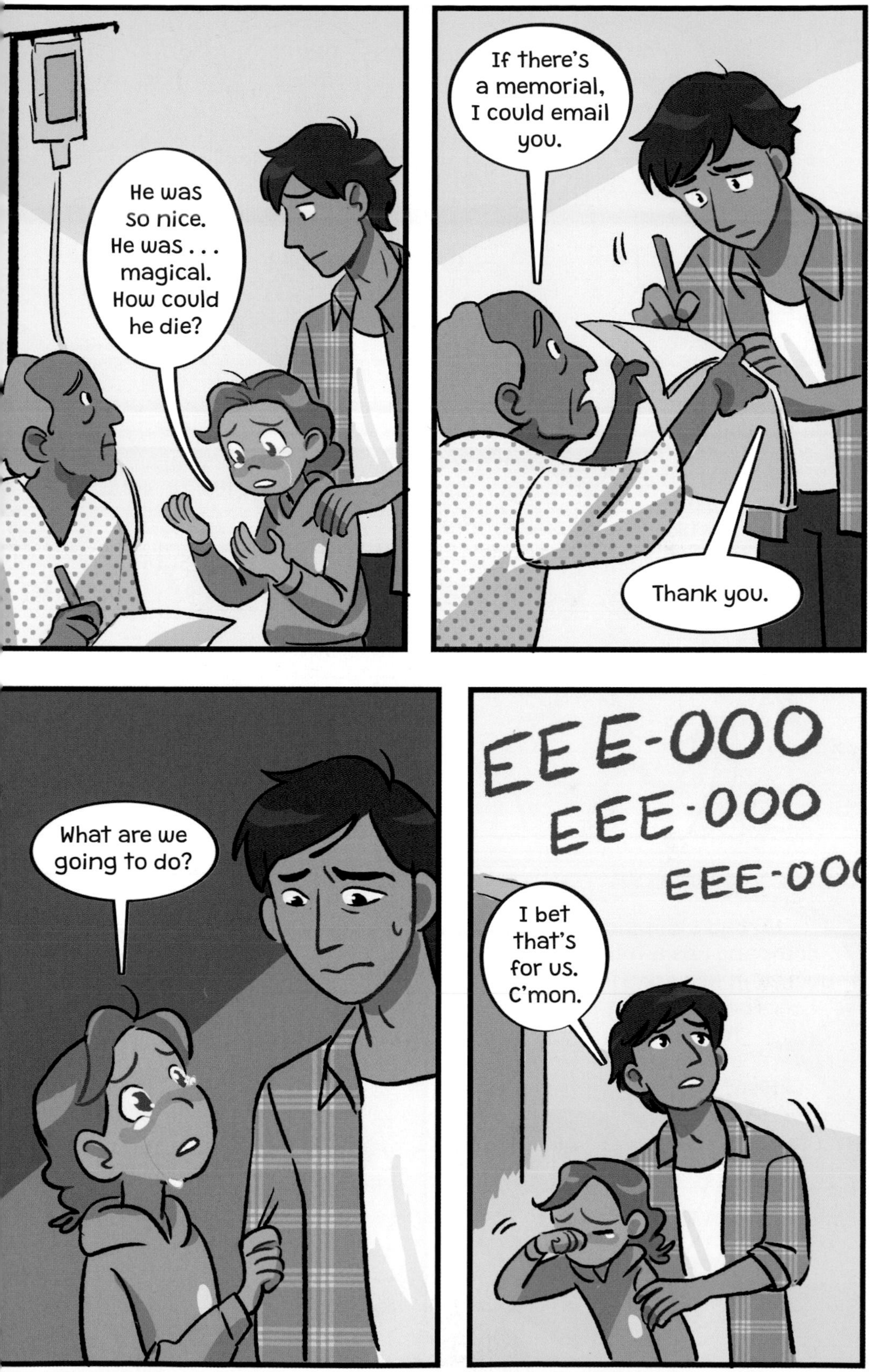
He was so nice. He was . . . magical. How could he die?
If there's a memorial, I could email you.
Thank you.
What are we going to do?
EEE-OOO
EEE-OOO
EEE-OOO
I bet that's for us. C'mon.

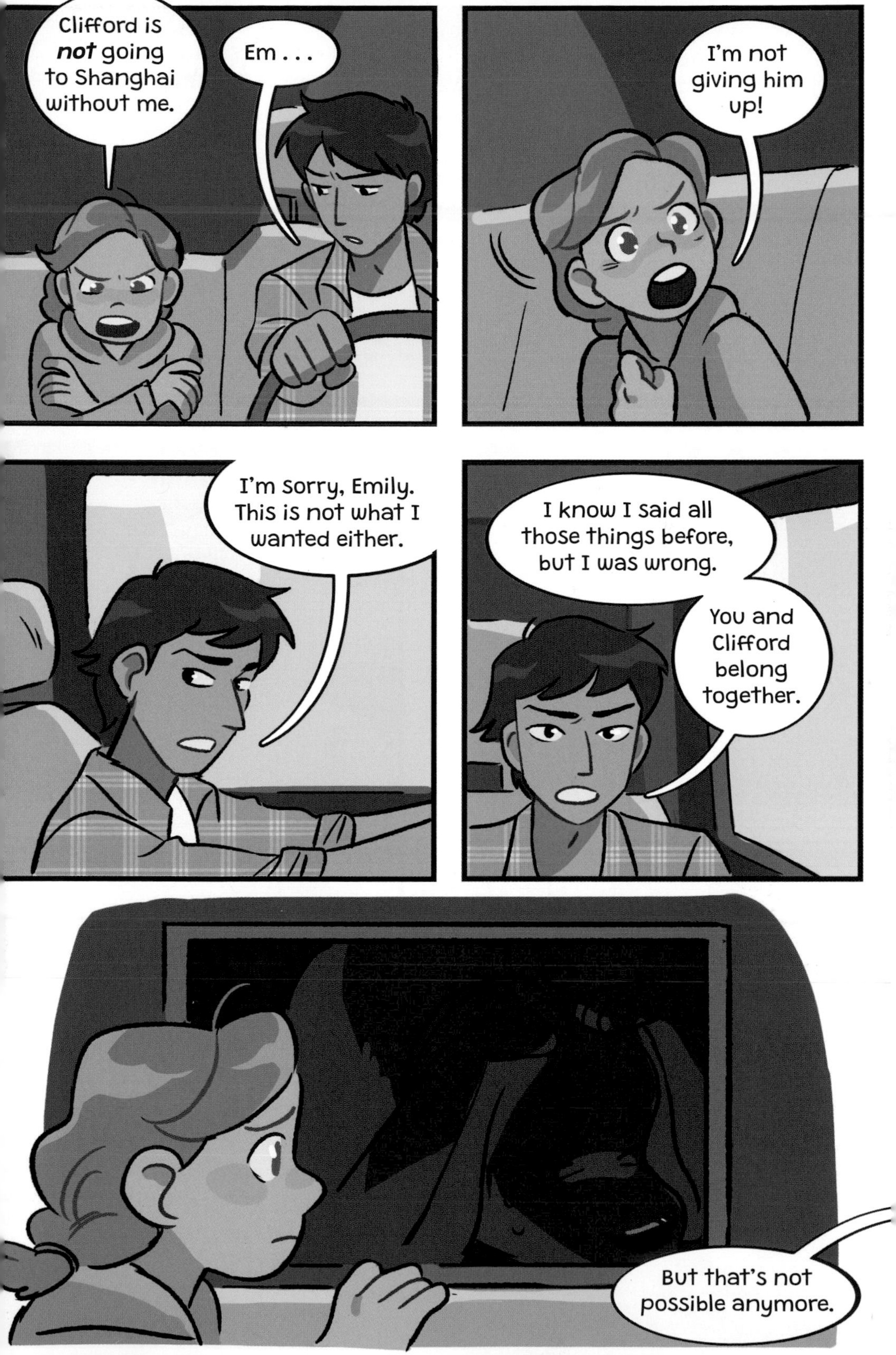

Clifford is ***not*** going to Shanghai without me.
Em . . .
I'm not giving him up!
I'm sorry, Emily. This is not what I wanted either.
I know I said all those things before, but I was wrong.
You and Clifford belong together.
But that's not possible anymore.

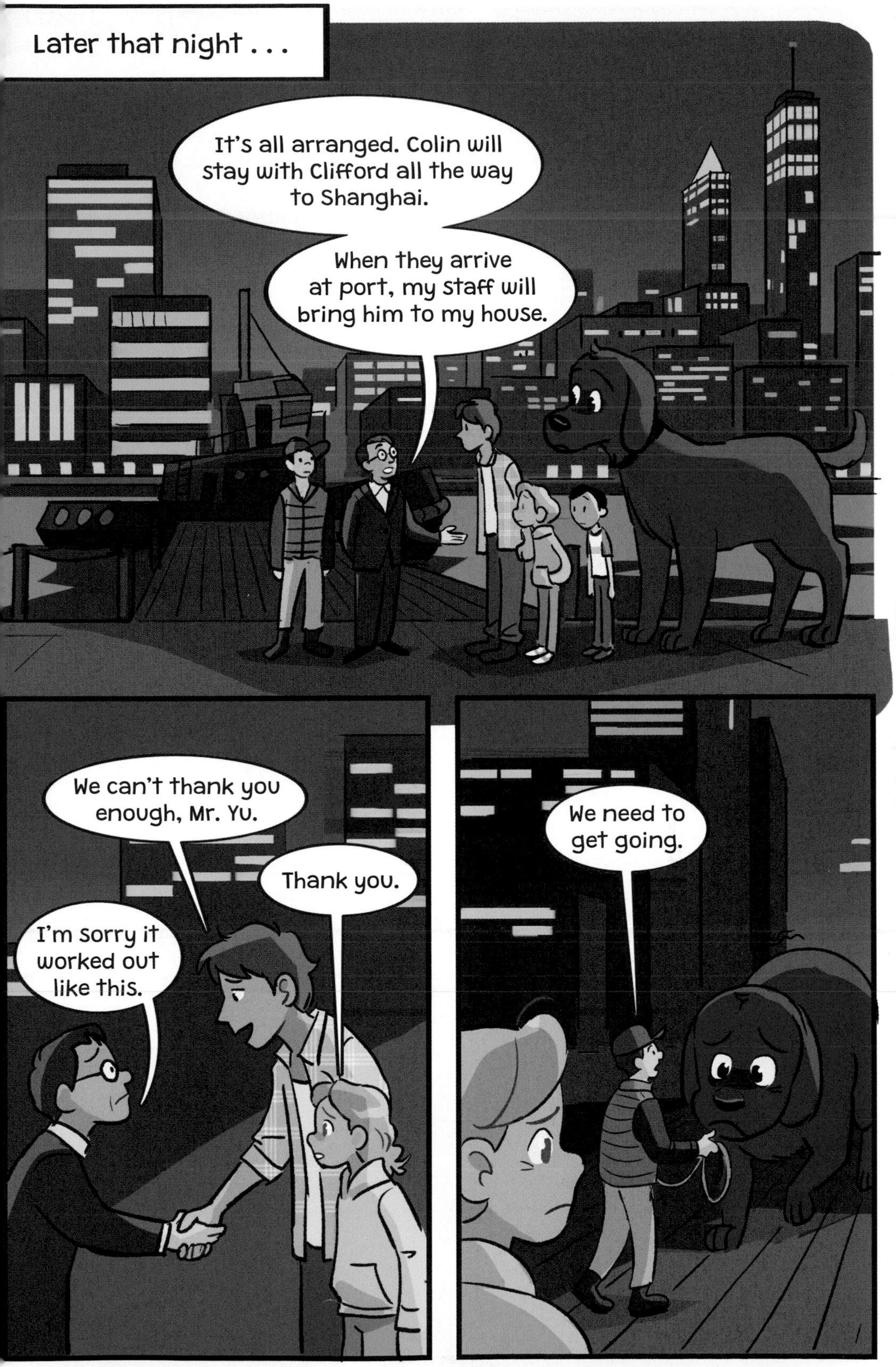
Later that night . . .
It's all arranged. Colin will stay with Clifford all the way to Shanghai.
When they arrive at port, my staff will bring him to my house.
We can't thank you enough, Mr. Yu.
Thank you.
I'm sorry it worked out like this.
We need to get going.

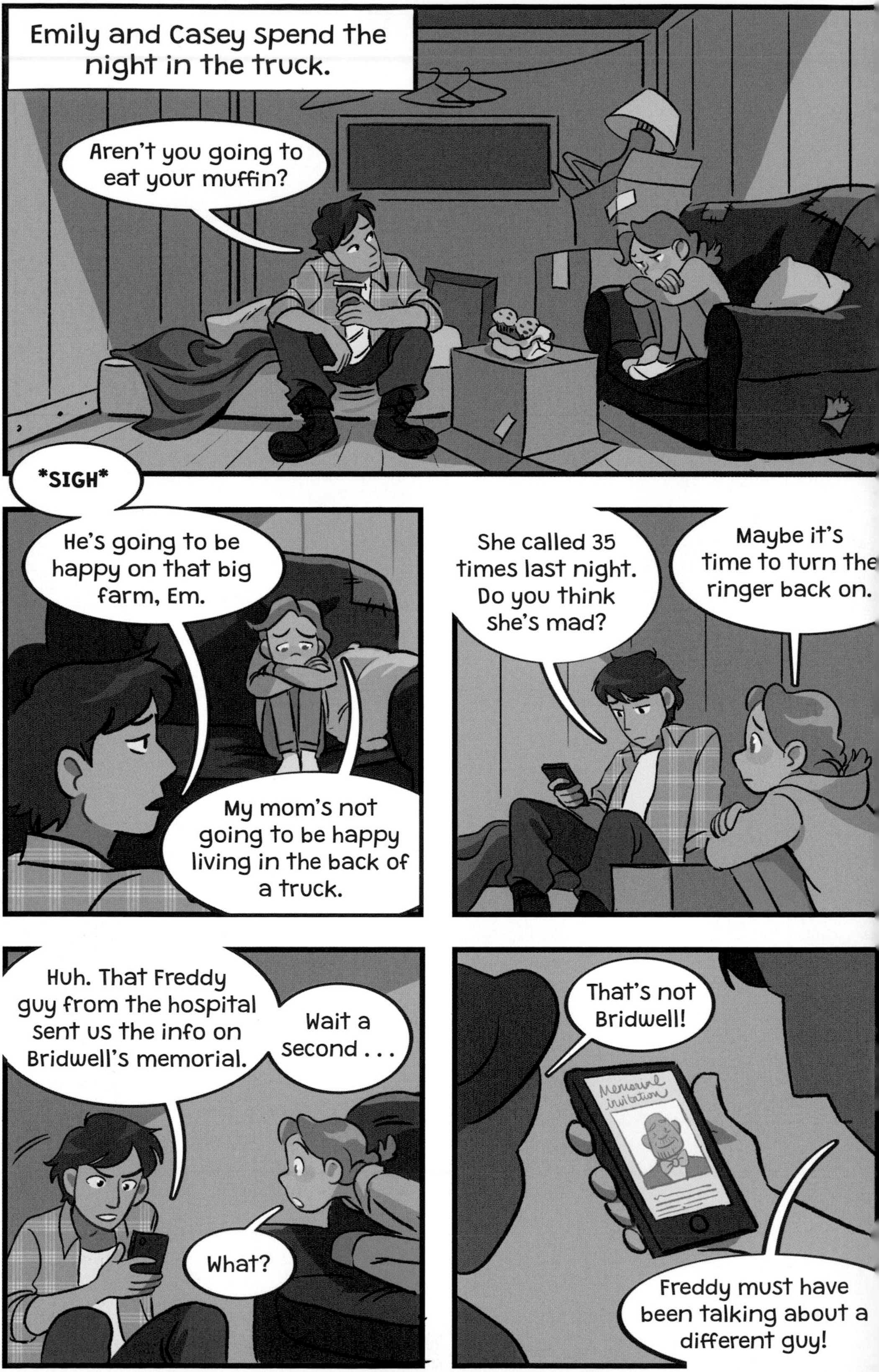
Emily and Casey spend the night in the truck.
Aren't you going to eat your muffin?
SIGH
He's going to be happy on that big farm, Em.
My mom's not going to be happy living in the back of a truck.
She called 35 times last night. Do you think she's mad?
Maybe it's time to turn the ringer back on.
Huh. That Freddy guy from the hospital sent us the info on Bridwell's memorial.
Wait a second . . .
What?
That's not Bridwell!
Memorial invitation
Freddy must have been talking about a different guy!

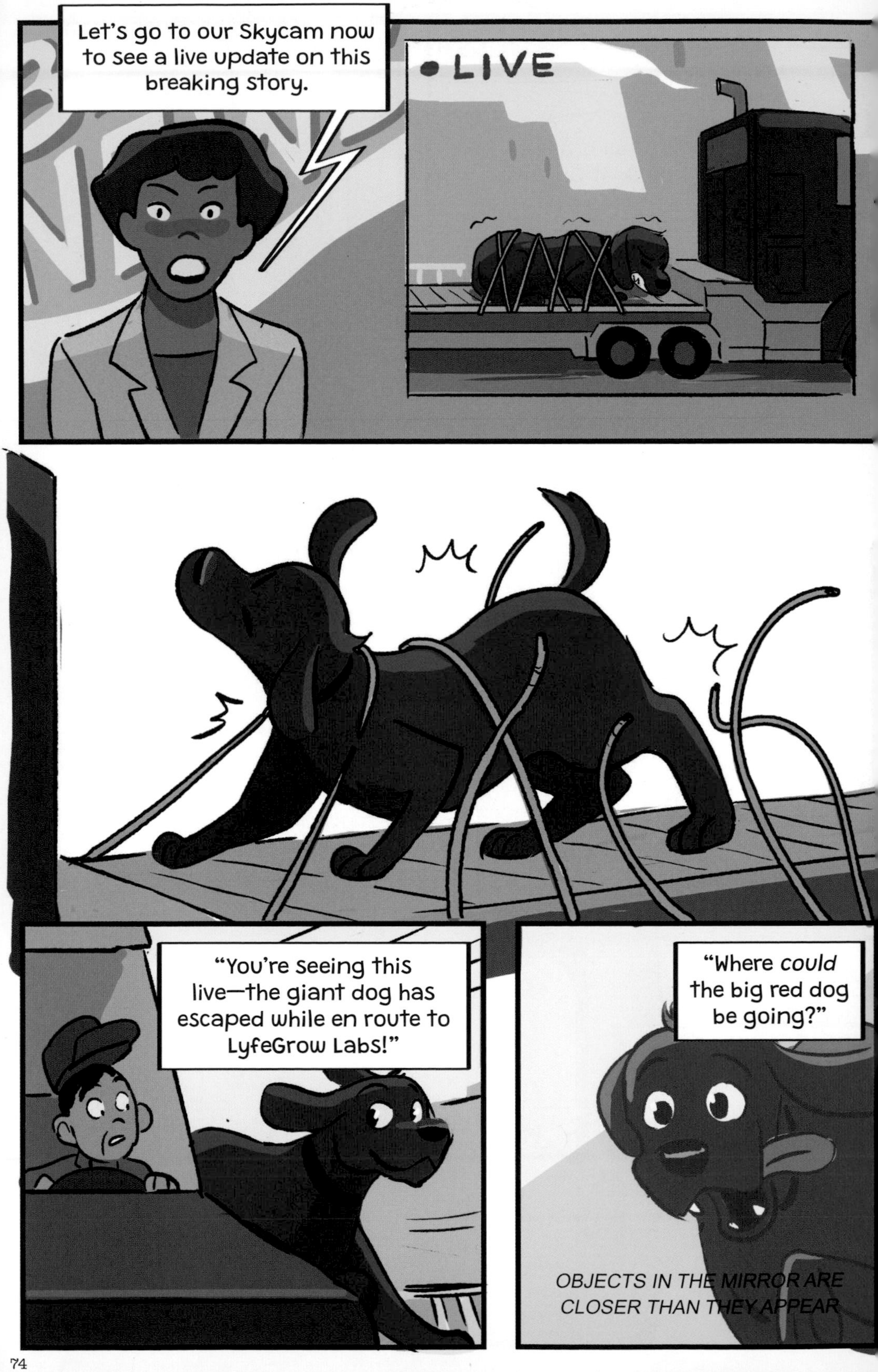
Let's go to our Skycam now to see a live update on this breaking story.
• LIVE
"You're seeing this live—the giant dog has escaped while en route to LyfeGrow Labs!"
"Where *could* the big red dog be going?"
OBJECTS IN THE MIRROR ARE CLOSER THAN THEY APPEAR

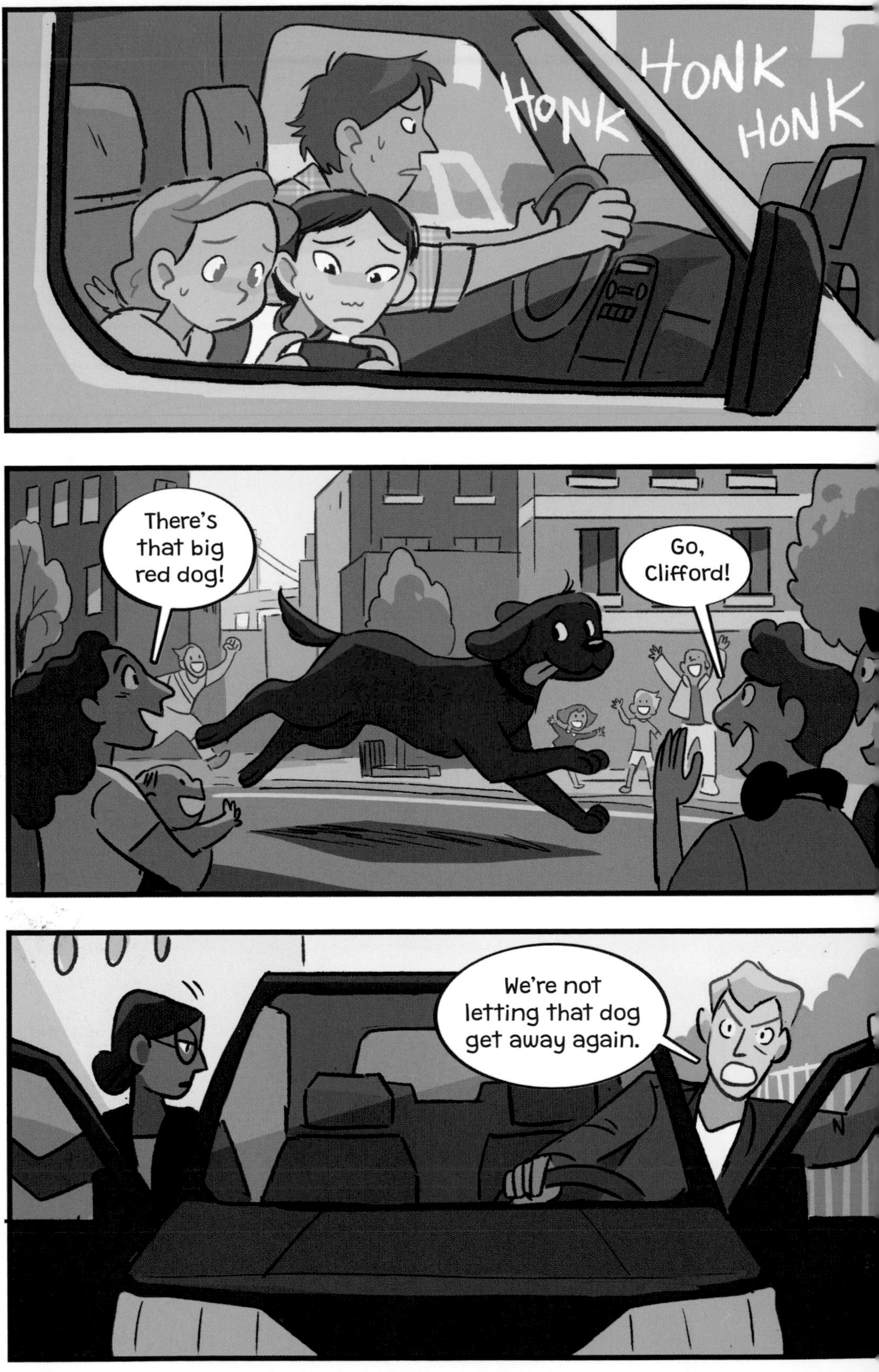
HONK
HONK
HONK
There's that big red dog!
Go, Clifford!
We're not letting that dog get away again.

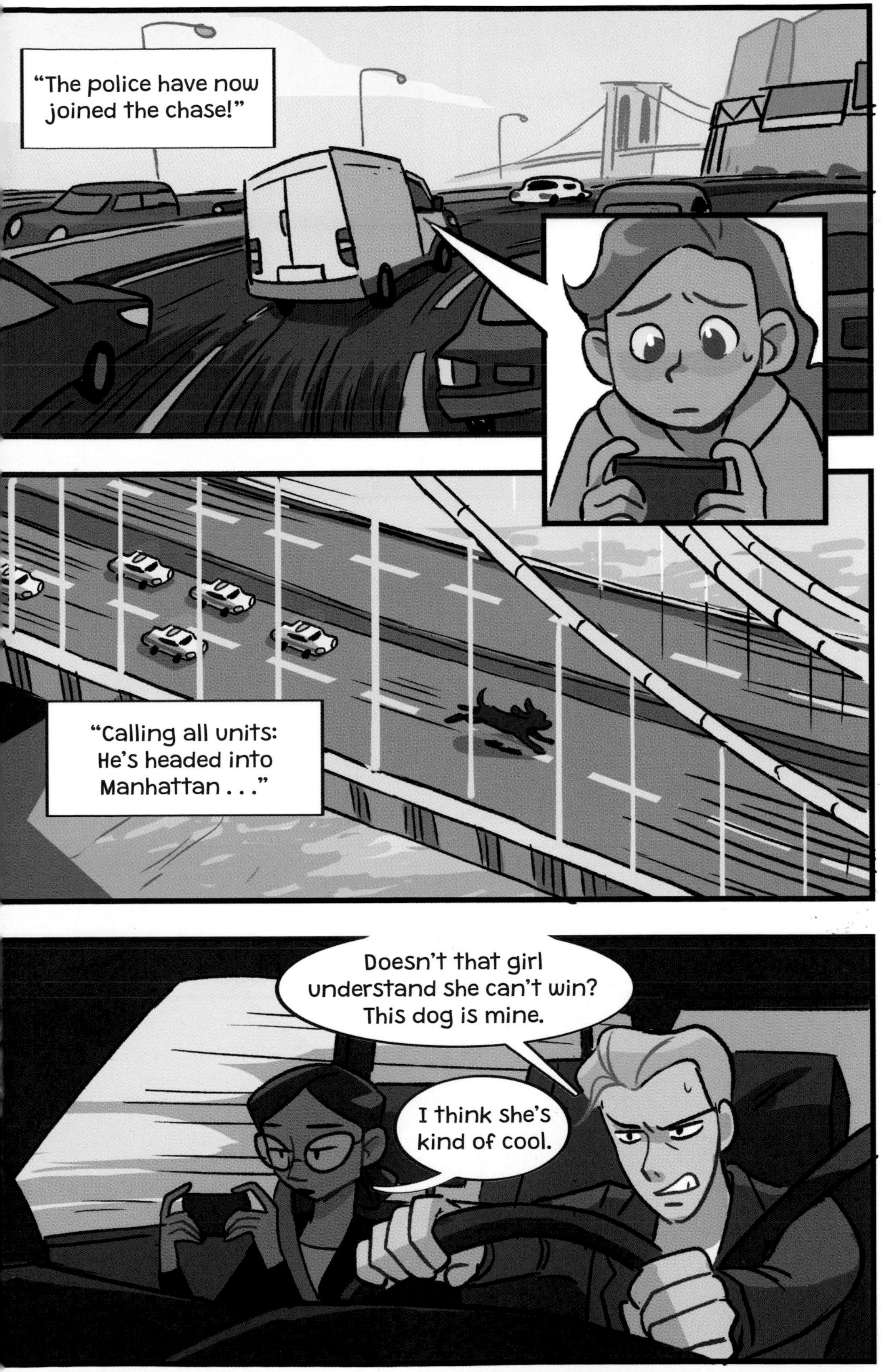
"The police have now joined the chase!"
"Calling all units: He's headed into Manhattan . . ."
Doesn't that girl understand she can't win? This dog is mine.
I think she's kind of cool.

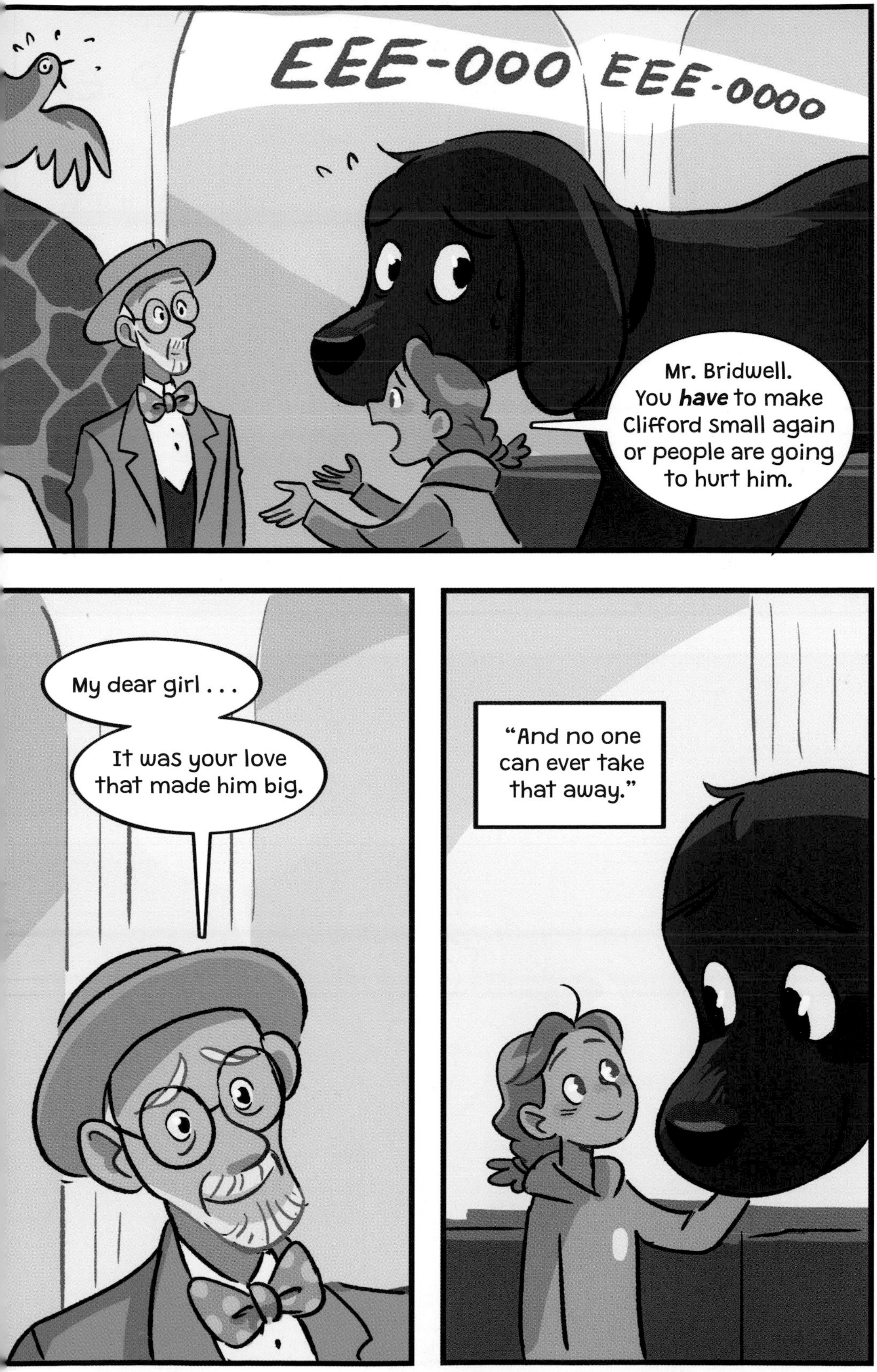
EEE-OOO EEE-OOOO
Mr. Bridwell. You ***have*** to make Clifford small again or people are going to hurt him.
My dear girl . . .
It was your love that made him big.
"And no one can ever take that away."

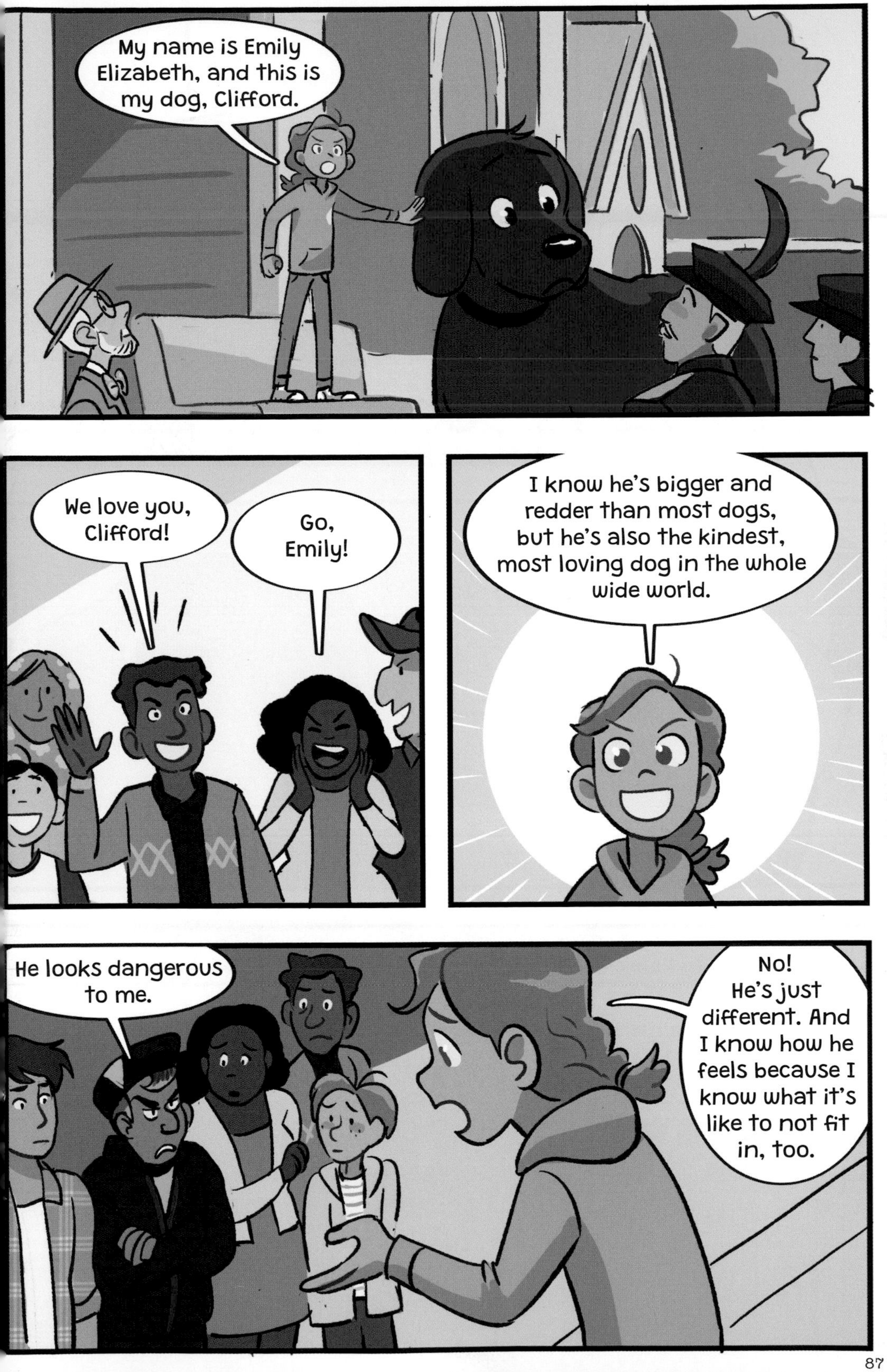
My name is Emily Elizabeth, and this is my dog, Clifford.
We love you, Clifford!
Go, Emily!
I know he's bigger and redder than most dogs, but he's also the kindest, most loving dog in the whole wide world.
He looks dangerous to me.
No! He's just different. And I know how he feels because I know what it's like to not fit in, too.

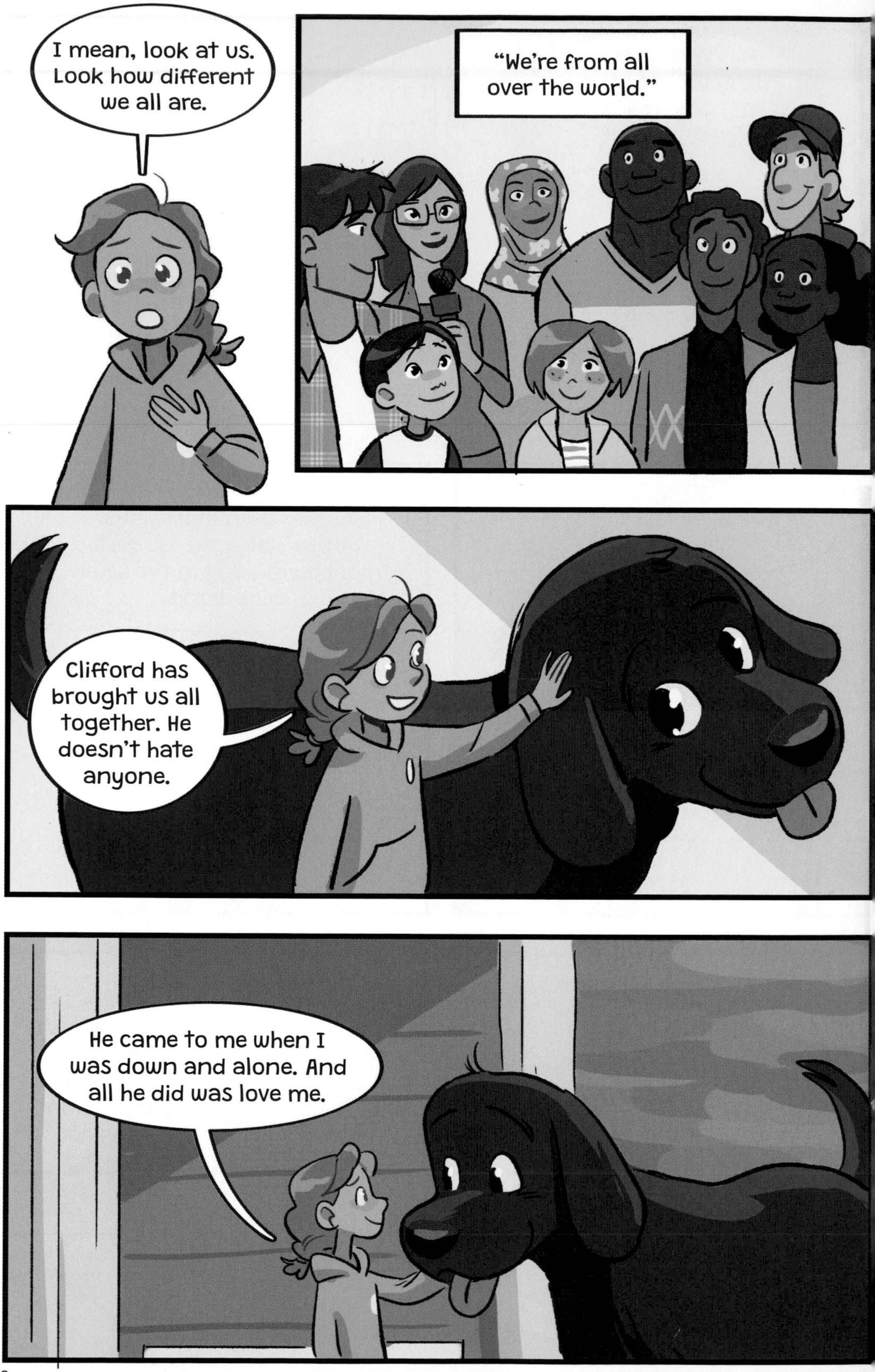
I mean, look at us. Look how different we all are.
"We're from all over the world."
Clifford has brought us all together. He doesn't hate anyone.
He came to me when I was down and alone. And all he did was love me.

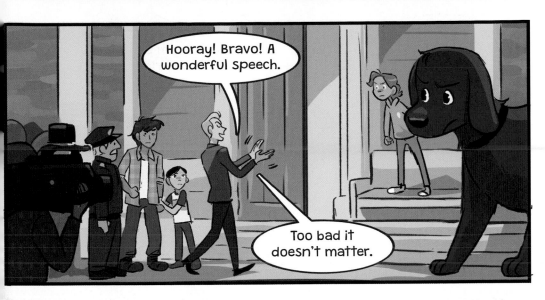

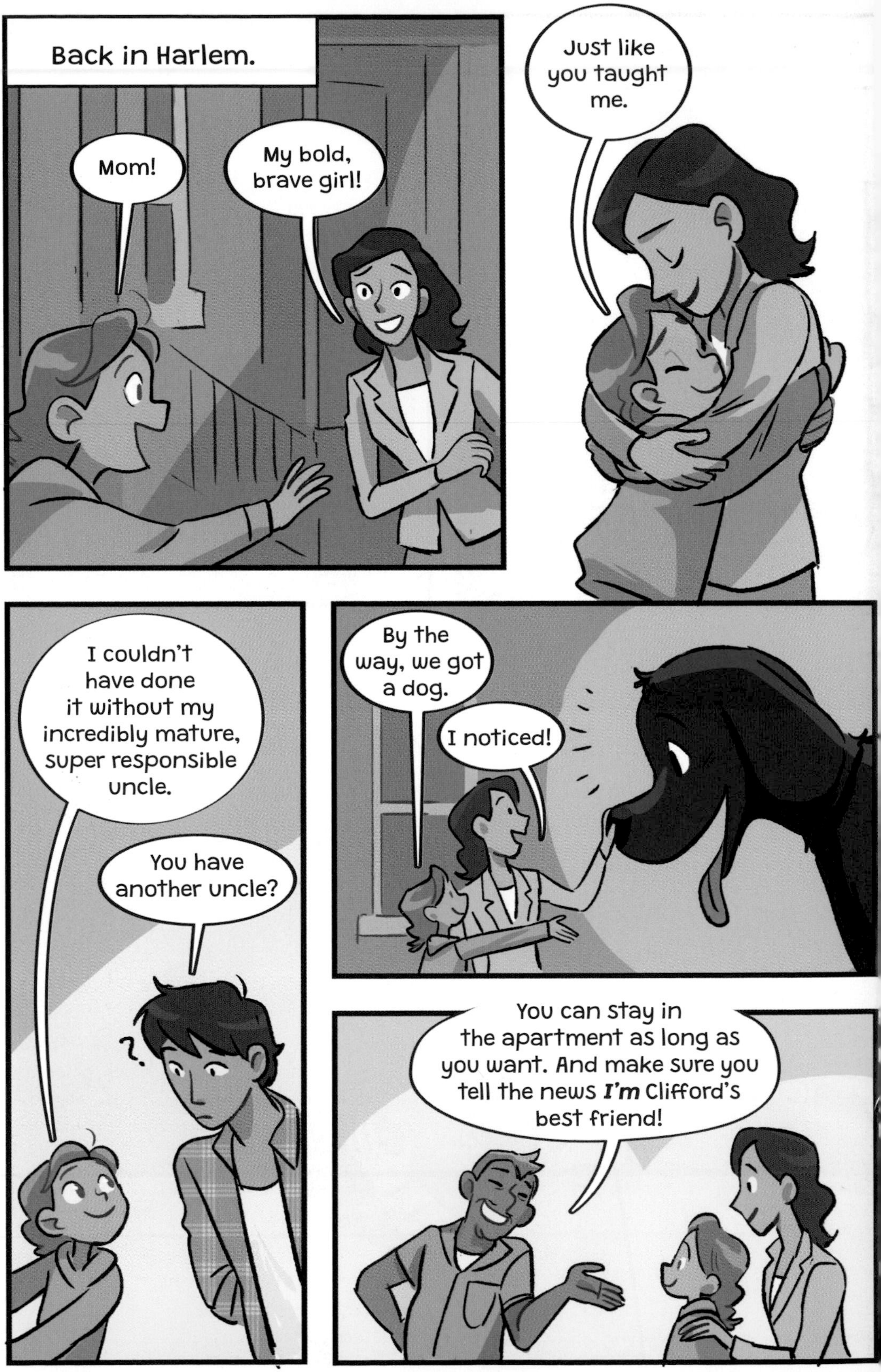
Back in Harlem.
Mom!
My bold, brave girl!
Just like you taught me.
I couldn't have done it without my incredibly mature, super responsible uncle.
You have another uncle?
By the way, we got a dog.
I noticed!
You can stay in the apartment as long as you want. And make sure you tell the news ***I'm*** Clifford's best friend!